TIM OLIVER, EVACUEE

To Emily

with love

Tom

11th March
2012.

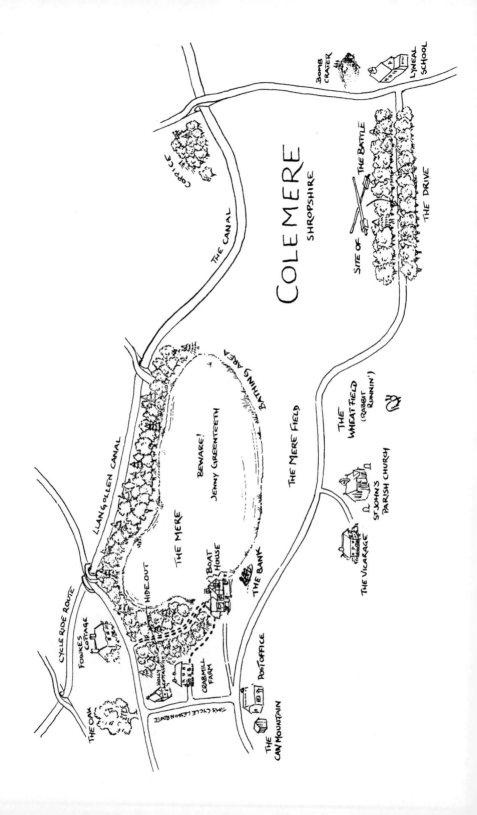

COLEMERE
SHROPSHIRE

TIM OLIVER
EVACUEE

BY
TOM FARRELL

Illustrated by
PETER ROGERS

A Bright Pen Book

British Library Cataloguing in Publication Data.
A catalogue record for this book is available from
the British Library.

ISBN 978-07552-14006

Authors OnLine Ltd
19 The Cinques
Gamlingay, Sandy
Bedfordshire SG19 3NU
England

This book is also available in e-book format, details
of which are available at www.authorsonline.co.uk
and also in paperback.

CONTENTS

CHAPTER ONE

AT WAR!

Tim scrambled up on top of the sandstone wall, found a smooth place to sit, and settled down to wait. Train-spotting was his favourite hobby, and this was a perfect position, with a great view of the Liverpool to Euston railway-line and the expresses as they picked up speed on their way south.

The wall ran for miles along an embankment which raised the line high up and level with the roofs of the houses in Welbeck Avenue, his street, so the passengers could easily look down on the little train-spotter with his notebook and pencil. The wall also brought the Avenue to a 'dead end'. It was one of hundreds laid out in straight lines all over the city of Liverpool, one of the world's great seaports, where the Olivers had lived ever since Tim's great, great grandfather had sailed across from Ireland in 1840.

Tim's Dad was a rope-maker, and, on visits to the factory, Tim loved watching hemp from India and sisal from Mexico being turned into all kinds of rope, from skipping rope for kids to massive, ten inch-thick mooring lines for ocean-going liners.

But this morning his mind was on trains. It was Sunday, so there weren't as many running as on weekdays; but the famous 'Coronation Scot' would be going by in a few minutes. Billy Thompson, his best friend, who lived just over the road, had a book about trains which said that it was the fastest express in the world, touching a hundred and fourteen miles an hour; and it was never late. Even if every other train was delayed, the Master at Lime Street station made sure that this one always left on time.

As he sat waiting patiently in the sunshine, he could easily imagine the fuss on Platform 1 – porters dashing about under the chief's eagle-eye, helping elderly passengers and ladies into their carriage, and slamming the door behind them with a loud 'calunk'; people arriving at the very last minute, all hot and bothered, half-walking, half-running, some with a little jump now and again, peering into every carriage hoping to find one with an untaken seat, and diving in at the very last moment.

Then, as the massive hands of the station clock moved to ten o'clock, with the shrill blast of a whistle, the flourish of a flag and a little lurch, the prince of steam would be on its way, up a slight gradient for the first half-mile, through towering sandstone cuttings, snaking and clattering across the maze of the 'Gridiron', the Edge Hill sidings, and out towards Wavertree, where the train-spotter sat waiting.

He listened for the hum on the lines which told him that it was approaching. Then, as it thundered past, he held his breath, and, to stop being blown off his perch, dug his heels into the wall.

He waved as usual, although he knew that the men on the foot-plate would probably be too busy getting up a 'head' of steam to wave back. But today he was in luck, as the driver poked his head out of the cab and waved his polishing rag. It was a bonus. Tim reckoned that he must be the luckiest train-spotter in the land, and wished that Billy had been in his usual place alongside him.

After all the excitement, he sat there enjoying the warm sunshine. It was the last day of the summer holidays and he wanted to make the most of it. But apart from a goods-train which seemed to trundle past forever, not much was happening. He guessed that the 'London, Midland and Scottish Railways' had decided to take it easy on this particular day.

It was Sunday September 3rd, 1939, a day that people would remember forever.

He slid down from his perch, rubbed his sandy fingers on his shorts and sauntered back down the Avenue to his house, number 6 in the long terrace of reddish-coloured houses with tiny front gardens and neat privet hedges.

Usually, on a day like this, a few of the residents would be outside chatting; but today they seemed to have decided to stay indoors for some reason or other, and the Avenue was strangely quiet.

The front door of number 6 was open and, as he wandered down the hallway, he called out...

"I'm home!"

There was no reply, but he could hear a voice. The wireless was on, and his Mum and Dad were sitting at the kitchen table listening. Shirley, his big sister, was half-listening, half-reading her Girls Crystal comic.

Dad spotted Tim in the doorway and put a finger to his lips.

The speaker sounded tired and very fed-up. He spoke slowly and quietly.

"...this country is now at war with Germany."

Shirley looked up from her comic and looked as if she might start to cry. Mum put her arms around her. Dad sat grim-faced.

"Why are we at war, Dad?" Tim asked.

"It's not our fault, Tim," he replied. "We warned Adolf Hitler - he's Germany's leader - that if Germany attacked Poland, we would stand by Poland. We're just keeping our promise."

"Why did they attack Poland?"

"Well, it's a long story...something to do with old grudges. Germany started the last war - that was the 1914-1918 war, the one that Granddad Oliver fought in - and when they were defeated, some of their land was taken away as a punishment. Now Hitler wants to take it back, and to grab more if he can. He's already taken over Austria and Czechoslovakia. His armies just marched over the borders without any warning and took charge."

Tim had heard the names, but had no idea where the places were.

Shirley was looking anxious.

"Will you have to join the army, Dad?"

"I'm probably too old, Shirley...and we must all hope the war will be over long before Tim's old enough to fight."

Tim frowned. He hadn't thought of that.

"Come on," said Mum, "the food's ready and we mustn't let Mr Hitler spoil our lunch."

But, as he munched, Tim was thinking dark thoughts about the bully who attacked other countries when they couldn't defend themselves, and he was glad that his country was keeping its promise, and sticking up for Poland.

Billy came over after lunch with Sid Shaw and Ken Cox, Tim's other 'best friends', and they went off to the park for football. They put their pullovers down for goal-posts and played shots-in; but it was very warm in the sunshine, and nobody wanted to be in goal anyway, so they sat in the goalmouth and chatted about the war.

"My Dad says that now we're at war with Germany, Hitler might send bombers to attack us," said Ken, "like he's attacked Poland. He says that all the kids will probably have to go away to the country, where it's safe."

"If we do, I hope we can go together," said Tim.

They all agreed, and sat around trying to imagine leaving home and living in the countryside, until Sid volunteered to be 'goalie'. They kicked the ball around for a few more minutes, then split up and went home.

Straightaway Tim noticed that his Mum's eyes were red and he could tell that she had been crying. Dad looked very solemn, and spoke quietly.

"The government says that, now that we're at war, it won't be safe for children to stay in cities and seaports, so they should be evacuated – that's sent away – to somewhere safe. Our city's bound to be a target for enemy bombers, with its docks and the shipbuilding yards over the water at Birkenhead."

"We've spoken on the telephone to Mrs Everson at Crab Mill Farm in Shropshire."

Mum had dried her eyes and was trying to sound cheerful.

"It's where I used to stay with Grandma in the summer holidays, when Grandpa Dodd took the scouts to camp. She says she'll be very happy to have you to stay, until it's safe to come back home."

But Shirley wasn't at all happy, and a big frown was spreading quickly across her face.

"Won't you be staying with us?"

"We wish we could," Mum replied, "but Dad's factory is making ropes for the Royal Navy now, so he must stay here, and he needs me to stay and look after him and our home."

The frown wasn't going away.

"We hate to have to send you away," said Dad, "but we want to be sure you're safe...and in any case, we hope the war will be over quite soon, and we can bring you back."

"Can't we go with our school friends?" It was Tim's turn to frown. "It'd be much more fun."

"I'm sure it would, Tim." Mum smiled. "But we think it'll be best for you to stay with someone we know; and Mr and Mrs Everson have got two children of their own, so you'll have plenty of fun."

"And we'll come down to visit as often as we can," Dad added.

"Will they give us our pocket money?" Tim asked.

"Yes, they will," Dad smiled, "...and when we hear that you've been on your best behaviour, Tim, there might be a bit extra!"

That cheered Tim up a bit, and he ran across to number 7 to tell Billy the news.

"Shirley and me're going to be 'vacuated."

"What's that?"

"It means we're going to go and live in the country – somewhere safe, like Sid said, in case the bombers come."

"Does that mean you won't have to go to school?"

"I hope so. Will you be 'vacuated, too?"

"I think so. Mum thinks I'll be going with the school, and she isn't very happy. She says the bombers might never come."

They stood uncertainly for a few moments.

"Anyway my Dad thinks the war won't last long," said Tim, "so we'll probably be back quite soon."

Billy wasn't so sure.

Soon after lunch the next day, the little black Morris belonging to Bill Brett, a friend of the family, turned slowly into Welbeck Avenue and pulled up outside number 6. It was quite old, 'almost vintage', Tim's Dad said, and creaked a bit when it started and stopped.

"But it's reliable," he said, and would take them safely to Crab Mill Farm.

The luggage, including a small pile of Tim's Beano comics, was loaded into the boot. His football wouldn't fit in, so he had to take it with him in the car wedged between his feet, which he thought was the right place for it, anyway. He and Shirley squeezed into the back seat with Mum, and Dad sat up-front to navigate.

By now quite a few of the neighbours had heard that the Oliver kids were being evacuated, and came to stand at their front door, looking sadly towards number 6.

"God bless!" they called out, "...and come back soon!"

Billy had already gone to school, but Tim spotted his Mum.

Mrs Thompson poked her head through the car window.

"Billy said to tell you 'Good luck', Tim, and don't forget to write a letter."

"I won't, Mrs Thompson...and say 'Cheerio' to Billy, please."

Suddenly he felt a bit sad himself. He hadn't thought much about going away and leaving Billy and the others behind; but now it was all happening, and Shropshire sounded a long way off.

Shirley sat quietly, holding her hanky and sniffing, but Tim waved through the back window as the car pulled away and headed out of the Avenue towards the city centre and into 'the tunnel'. The King had come specially to open the Mersey Tunnel only four years before, so it was almost brand new, and Tim thought it was a pity to be saying goodbye to it already.

They came out into bright sunshine and drove past ship-building yards, where the giant cranes were already being painted grey and green to keep enemy bombers guessing, and soon they were chugging along steadily through the sleepy county of Cheshire towards the even sleepier county of Shropshire. Everything seemed quite peaceful, not the least bit like wartime.

A bigger car full of children swept past, and a boy grinned at Tim as if to say 'our car's faster than yours'. Tim put his thumb to his nose and wiggled his fingers in return. Shirley frowned.

"Don't do that, Tim!"

"D'you think they're being 'vacuated too, Mum," asked Tim.

"I expect so."

"I wonder where they'll be staying?"

There was no reply. Mum was deep in sad thought.

At Whitchurch they turned west and the speed dropped, as the roads became narrower. A tractor pulling a cart loaded high with hay slowed them down, but at last they reached Colemere, a tiny village tucked away in the countryside, north of the ancient market town of Shrewsbury.

Now they meandered slowly along single-track lanes in between high earth-banks and hedges, and finally turned by the village pump into a lane which dropped down to their destination, Crab Mill Farm.

There were potholes everywhere, so the Everson family had heard them coming, and by the time they had creaked to a halt by the garden gate, they had formed a line to greet them.

"This is your country family," whispered Mum, "so try to look happy, everyone!" But that was almost impossible for Shirley, who had never felt so sad.

Tim was more curious than sad, and while hands were being shaken, he was looking at his country family. Farmer Everson was wearing his suit, which he only ever wore for special occasions, and a floppy, brown hat which, Tim discovered, he wore almost all the time. He had strong, gnarled hands, a friendly, sunburnt face and a surprisingly quiet voice for a farmer, Tim thought.

Their new 'Mum' was friendly-looking, too. She was quite plump, and wearing a pinafore over her cheerful, flowery dress, as if she had just emerged from the kitchen.

Muriel, his new 'sister', was just a bit older than Shirley. She was wearing spectacles, like her Mum, and he thought she looked very clever.

She stepped forward, smiling.

"Hello, Shirley...I'm Muriel. Welcome to Crab Mill!"

Shirley tried to smile back. "Thank you. Mum has told me what a nice place it is."

So far there was no sign of Joe. Then, suddenly, he burst through the garden gate with the farm dog at his heels. He was only a few months older than Tim, but a few inches taller. His face was covered with freckles, and very red from running.

"Joe...this is Tim." said his Mum.

"Hello, Tim," he grinned, "...sorry I wasn't here to meet you." He pointed to the dog, "Shep and me were stalkin' rabbits in the top field."

"Pleased to meet you, Joe" said Tim, as politely as he knew how. "I think I'd enjoy that."

"It's fun," said Joe, "...but they're tricky things to catch, I can tell you, even with a dog."

Mrs Everson smiled. "I don't think you need worry about your Tim," she said to his Mum. "He and Joe are already talking like old friends!"

Everyone was invited into the living room for tea, with scones, home-made damson jam and cream, while the grown-ups chatted about things like pocket-money, tooth brushing, bed-time and 'lights out'.

By now Shirley had had time to have a good look at her new country 'sister'. Muriel had short blond hair and brown eyes and spoke with a soft 'country' accent, unlike the chirpy, sing-song way that Liverpool girls talked.

After tea she led the way upstairs. "We'll be sharing my room," she said. "...I hope that's alright." She had emptied two drawers and pointed to them.

"They're for you."

"Thank you," Shirley replied very quietly, and began to empty her suitcase neatly into the drawers. She was still feeling glum, and Muriel couldn't help noticing.

"It must be awful to have to leave your home and say good-bye to your Mum and Dad," she said.

"Yes...and my friends too," Shirley replied, so quietly that Muriel could hardly hear the words, "...but my Dad says it's better to be safe than sorry if the bombing starts."

Muriel wanted to cheer her up. "Well, it's quite an adventure for Joe and me, having you and your brother as a part of our family."

"I just hope Tim behaves himself." Shirley was almost talking to herself now. "He's always in trouble at home."

Tim had followed Joe upstairs and into his room. It was at the very end of the farmhouse, and from the window he could see the sheds across a yard where the cows were being milked.

He bundled his clothes into the drawer which Joe's Mum had emptied for him, and rolled his football under the bed.

"Do you play football, Joe?" he asked.

"Yes, we do a bit; but our school's very small, so we haven't got a team ...or a pitch."

"That's hard luck," said Tim, who couldn't imagine a school without a football pitch.

It was almost time for Mum and Dad to head back to Liverpool, and the boys hurried downstairs.

"Now don't you worry!" Mrs Everson was saying to Mrs Oliver. "They'll be fine."

But, as she hugged Tim, Mum was trying her hardest not to worry.

"Now, Tim Oliver, you be on your best behaviour." Dad spoke

quietly, so that no one else could hear. "Do as you're told, and make your Mum and me proud of you when we come to visit."

Tim nodded. He had never been away from his Mum and Dad for more than a few hours, and couldn't imagine living all the time in someone else's house. He thought he was going to cry, but wasn't going to do that in front of his new family, so he chewed his lip instead.

Then the car was heading off up the lane towards the pump and Liverpool, Mum crying quietly in the back seat, Dad just staring straight ahead, and Bill Brett steering in silence.

The Eversons stood together waving, as the Morris disappeared from sight, and the last they heard of it was a faint crash as it went over a pothole.

Shirley held Tim's hand for a few moments.

Now they were evacuees.

CHAPTER TWO

COLEMERE

"Time to get up, everyone! Breakfast in ten minutes."

Tim opened his eyes and everything felt odd. It wasn't just the new bedroom and a strange voice calling them for breakfast. He liked the room. It was brightly painted, with pictures of aeroplanes and fighting ships on the walls. But it was Joe's room, not his. And Mrs Everson seemed very nice; but she was Joe's Mum.

And he wasn't the only one feeling a bit odd.

Joe had never shared his room with someone else, except when his cousin Eddie came to stay, and they usually quarrelled, so he didn't stay long. But this funny little city boy had come to stay for good.

They had finished breakfast, and Mrs Everson looked across the table at her new family members.

"Now, Shirley and Tim, I've spoken with Mrs Low, the Headmistress at the school. I told her that I have two perfectly behaved evacuees staying at Crab Mill Farm, and hope she can make room for two more pupils."

Tim frowned.

"D'you mean we've got to go to school?"

Now Shirley frowned.

Mrs Everson chuckled.

"You didn't think it would be a good idea to stay here with the ducks and cows, while everyone else was learning their lessons at school, did you, Tim?"

"I just thought there mightn't be enough space for us." He meant that he 'hoped' there 'wouldn't' be enough space for him.

"Well, Mrs Low says she will do her best to fit you in. I'll

take you tomorrow."

The next morning they set off with Mrs Everson, past the village church and up the road which linked Colemere to Lyneal, the neighbouring village.

'The Drive' ran straight for more than a quarter of a mile through an avenue of horse-chestnut trees. The branches arched over to meet each other like a tunnel, and looming up at the far end stood the school. It was built of red brick, with smallish windows, a clock over the door and a little bell on the roof. To Tim it looked like a prison, and the railings around the playground made him think of a cage.

As they walked into the playground a group of pupils stared at him. He thought of pulling tongues, but stared back instead, and followed Mrs Everson into the school. It was just one big room divided by a partition, and filled with very old desks. There was the same strange smell - of floor-polish and ink-wells, he guessed - as the classrooms at Dovedale Road School back at home. He supposed that it must be the same in all schools and didn't like it, probably because he didn't like school.

The Headmistress emerged from her office, which was also the school kitchen.

Mrs Drusilla Low had been the Headmistress of Lyneal school for a very long time, in fact almost since before anyone could remember, and, according to Joe, she was very strict. She strode across to meet the new pupils with long, stately steps, as if she was sailing, holding her head high and lips pressed tightly together, as if she found it difficult to smile.

Tim's heart sank.

"Here are the two evacuees I told you about, Mrs Low," said Mrs Everson, "...Shirley and Tim Oliver."

The Headmistress looked at Shirley and smiled slightly. Then she looked at Tim and frowned. Tim looked at his feet. He noticed that one of his stockings had fallen down; but he couldn't pull it up because, at that moment, his fingers were crossed in the desperate hope that there wasn't enough room for two extra pupils – or at least one, in which case Shirley would surely be chosen, because, as everyone knows, girls are always the keenest pupils.

"Well," said Mrs Low in an official 'in charge' voice, "my school already has too many pupils, now that the evacuees have arrived... but I suppose you can't just stay at Crab Mill Farm all day long, can you?"

Shirley glared at Tim as if to say 'Don't dare answer!'

Tim said nothing, but kept his fingers crossed.

The Headmistress went on "As you can see, all the desks are taken, so you will have to sit at the back until we can find some more. Shirley, you will be in Miss Beddoes' class, and Timothy," she looked down at him and frowned again; "...you will be in class one...my class."

His heart sank lower.

But the news wasn't all bad. The back of the class was his favourite place, where he would hardly be noticed; and class one was Joe's class, so they would be together.

Mrs Everson smiled encouragingly at him, said 'Good morning' to the Headmistress, and left him to his fate. He took his place on a bench at the back of the class and spent the rest of the morning looking around at his new classmates. Most of them seemed very little, rather noisy, and a bit of a nuisance. Mrs Everson had explained that some country village schools didn't have many children, so five-to-eight year-olds were all put together in the same class with one teacher. It was the same with the nines-to-elevens.

"I don't think Mrs Low likes having the evacuees," said Joe. They were on their way down The Drive after school.

Tim nodded sadly. "Especially boys."

****

Crab Mill Farm lay on a ridge of high ground. On one side of the ridge the land fell away steeply through a wood of beeches, elms and firs to a big lake. On the other side it sloped more gently towards the village centre.

It was mainly a dairy farm, sending milk daily to the depot in Ellesmere, the nearest town. There were chickens which had the freedom of the farm, and a few ducks which seemed to spend all their time nose-diving in the pond and generally making a mess of feathers and poo on the banks. Tim wondered why Mr Everson bothered with them, except that they looked quite nice just floating about.

Then there was Sheriff, the carthorse. He was a 'chestnut', fifteen hands high according to Joe, with a wonderful mane that anybody would want to brush, and matching tail. He wasn't noted for his speed, but, when extra muscle was needed for pulling things, especially at harvest time, he was always the star performer, and it was Joe's job to keep him well-fed, 'watered', and brushed down.

Lastly there was Shep. He was technically a sheep dog, which was how he got his name. But as the farm had no sheep, and the cows took no notice of him, he had turned his attention to the local rabbits. However he was getting on in years, and tended to wheeze as he approached his prey; so he was absolutely hopeless at catching them.

Back at the farm the boys polished off a plate of bread and jam; then Joe said "Come on, I'll show you the mere," and, without any warning, he set off across the main yard, through a gate and onto a footpath across a field leading to a stile. Once over that, Tim found himself at the top of a slope which dropped down to the edge of the lake.

"Follow me!" Joe shouted, and started half-running, half-sliding down the slope.

"The mere," he said, pointing with his chin towards the lake. With one hand on the ground for balance, he led the way down through the branches of beech trees which reached almost to the ground, like giant curtains. They slithered down the last few yards and came to a sudden halt, close to a black and white building perched right on the edge of the mere.

"The boathouse," said Joe, to save Tim the trouble of asking.

"Come on!" he yelled, dashing around to the front, where a slightly rickety, wooden jetty ran out into the mere, a few yards from the entrance to the boathouse. An inlet allowed the water to run under where the upper floor of the house jutted out, supported by two pillars, and inside, swaying about in slow motion as the water lapped up to them, were two boats. They were like rowing boats, with rowlocks

and oars, but had square ends, deep sides and flat bottoms.

"Punts!" Joe explained, in case a city boy couldn't recognise them.

"What are they for?" asked the city boy, who had already guessed that they must be something to do with fishing, but was hoping that, if he asked a good question, his guide might say a whole sentence or two in reply. But no such luck.

"Fishin'!" said Joe. "Come on...let's see if old Sam's at home."

"Who's old Sam?"

"You'll see. He's in charge here...he looks after the mere and the boathouse. He knows everythin' about the meres."

He led the way around to the side door and knocked.

"You mean there's more than one?"

While they waited, the guide answered.

"Oh yes. There's lots...Ellesmere, Kettlemere, Crowsmere, Whitemere, Blakemere...and a few others. Ellesmere's the biggest and most important 'cos it's next to the Town. But Colemere's nearly as big, I think."

They stood waiting, then picked up the sound of muttering.

Joe grinned.

"That'll be Sam. He chats to himself sometimes!"

There was a grating noise as a bolt was drawn, the door opened slowly, and standing there, peering at them over a pair of very thick spectacles, was one of the smallest 'grown-ups' Tim had ever seen.

He wasn't much taller than Joe, but much broader, with large muscles. He had a little beard on the end of his chin, and very bright, dark-brown eyes which his spectacles made look extra-large. A beret was perched on the back of his head, and he reminded Tim of a picture he had seen of Rumpelstilskin.

"Good day, Sam," said Joe, pulling Tim forward.

"This is Tim...he's an evacuee."

The boathouse keeper looked at Tim and touched his forehead, as if he was meeting a very important person.

"Good day, Joe," he said, "...and good day to you, young sir," he smiled. "And where are you from, may I ask?"

"Liverpool, sir" replied Tim.

"Well now," said Sam, "...many years ago boy scouts used to camp at Colemere. They were from Liverpool. They pitched their tents over there on the mere-field."

He pointed to a wide, grassy area between the mere and the village church.

"My Grandpa..." Tim wanted to say something, but the old chap didn't want to stop.

"They were a lively lot. I got back from market one day and there, out in the middle, was one of my punts full of the little imps, shoutin' an' splashin' enough to turn it over!"

"Well, I can tell you, I were very worried in case some of 'em fell in and couldna' swim. I were angry too, wondrin' what were happenin' to my punt. I waved my stick at 'em, and shouted to 'em to come back at once. They could tell I were angry. They stopped their shoutin' and splashed their way back in a great hurry.'

"Boy scouts are supposed to be sensible," I said.

"'Sorry, mister,' they said. 'We were playing pirates.'"

He chuckled.

"Well, they were a nice lot of lads...and I were a lad myself once."

Joe looked at Tim and pulled a face. It was difficult to imagine old Sam as a 'lad'!

Sam took no notice, and went on... "I said I believed 'em, and sent 'em back to the camp. The scout-master came to see me. He said there was goin' to be a camp-fire that evenin', but, as a punishment, 'the pirates' wouldn't be allowed to join in. He were a good scout-master, Mr Dodd...a gentleman."

He stopped speaking for a moment, and Tim had his chance to interrupt.

"That was my Grandpa, sir!" he said, proudly. "He used to bring my Mum to the camp when she was a girl. She stayed with Grandma at Crab Mill Farm and helped at the camp, setting the tables and peeling the potatoes."

"I believe I remember her!" said Sam. "A pretty young lady with long, black hair. She were very popular with the boys, I think!" He winked.

Tim grinned. "She's very pretty now, sir!"

"Tell Tim about the meres and the legends, please, Sam." It was Joe's turn to interrupt.

The old chap tugged at his beard.

"Oh, I can tell you strange things about the meres. They inna' like or'nary lakes…just great holes in the ground. They say they were filled with ice once, and when the ice thawed, the water was left to form the meres. They dunna' get their water from a river, and they're very deep. Folks say there's no bottom to 'em, and that's why the water's so cold. Then there are the bells. They say they were thrown into Colemere by wicked hands long ago. They dunna' say why, and if they were church bells. People say they can still be heard ringin'. I dunna' know if it's true. I anna' ever 'eard 'em myself, although I've listened, specially when it's very quiet and still of an evenin'."

Tim frowned. He was trying to work out how bells could be heard ringing under water

"Perhaps someone will try to find them one day, sir, with a mini-submarine…or something like that."

"Maybe they will," replied Sam. "I dunna' know about that. It's very dark down there. I think it's best to leave 'em alone." He looked out across the smooth surface of the mere.

"Tell him about Jenny, Sam," said Joe.

"Oh, you mean Jenny Greenteeth, the strange lady who's supposed to live in the meres…you might say she's a 'mere-maid'!" He chuckled at his little joke.

"Well, I've lived among the meres for seventy years and I anna' ever seen 'er, and I dunna' know if I want to. So whether she 'as green teeth or not, I canna' say. The story is that she lives among the rushes, and if children venture too close to the water's edge she'll try to catch 'em and drag 'em in."

He noticed that Tim was glancing anxiously at the water.

"But it's only a legend," he added quickly, smiling. "We dunna' want your young city friend 'avin' bad dreams, Joe!"

Joe laughed. "If I hear him screamin' in his sleep, I'll know he's dreamin' about Jenny! But we've got to go now, Sam...thanks for the stories."

"Yes, thanks, sir," Tim added, with another quick glance towards the nearest rushes, as they left the story-teller to his punts and memories.

CHAPTER THREE

CAMPS AND CANS

"Does he live in the boathouse all by himself?" Tim asked, as Joe led the way through a gate towards the open space which Sam had called the 'mere-field'.

"Yes. He anna' got a family of his own...'cept us! We all call him Sam, so you should!" .

He pointed to the field.

"Sam says the Cavaliers' army camped here once...three thousand of 'em. They were on the King's side in the civil war. It was a safe place to camp, flat and open, so they couldna' be surprised."

Tim nodded. He had seen pictures of the Cavaliers and Roundheads.

Now Joe pointed to the far end of the field.

"That's where we swim when the cows anna' there. It's shallow, and quite warm in the summer."

He pointed to the church which stood on slightly higher ground.

"That's the parish church. We share it with Lyneal, like the school. My Dad does little jobs there like ringin' the bell and blowin' the bellows for the organ. He's called the verger...I'm not sure why. Sometimes I help him shovellin' the coke, to keep the church warm. Mr Pye's the vicar. He's a good cricketer, and my Mum says he's quite a good preacher, too. That's the vicarage next door."

The mere-field sloped steeply up from the edge of the mere towards the village, and Joe pointed.

"We sledge there when there's snow; you can get up real speed; but you've got to be careful not to go onto the ice, unless old Sam says you can."

The rest of the field was flat. Gorse bushes, with their bright yellow flowers, and a few hollows were the only things that broke up the flatness.

Now Tim was trying to imagine hundreds of tents in neat rows, the Cavaliers with their high boots, broad-brimmed hats and feathers, practising fencing, and the King's banners fluttering in the cool breeze coming off the water.

Then, in his imagination, he 'fast-forwarded' to another camp scene, three hundred years after the Cavaliers. It was an army of excited city lads. They were in uniform, too – brown shirts, the green and black 'neckerchiefs' of the 15th Anfield, St Simon and St Jude's church troop, and strange-shaped hats – busy tying different kinds of knots, waving flags to send messages, and lighting fires without matches; and, setting the tables for supper, a pretty, dark-haired girl, named Margery, who would one day be his Mum.

He thought about her now, with no children to look after, and number 6 all quiet. She would probably be feeling lonely, he guessed, and made up his mind to write a letter.

"Come on!" Joe interrupted his day-dream, and headed up the bank towards the village centre.

"What does 'dunna' mean?" Tim asked.

Joe grinned. "It's how we say 'don't... and we say canna' for can't, and 'wonna' for 'won't... so can you guess what 'munna' means?"

Tim thought hard. "Is it 'mustn't'?"

"Right!" Joe laughed. "There's a saying...'You munna' say dunna' it inna' polite'. D'you get it?"

Tim spoke slowly..."You mustn't say 'dunna', it isn't polite."

"Right first time, Tim! You'll soon be talkin' like us."

By now they had reached the first houses in the village, and Joe turned into a lane leading to another black and white building with a notice over the door -

COLEMERE POST OFFICE

He pressed the latch and pushed the door open. A bell tinkled, and, as they went in, Tim's nose told him that it wasn't just a Post Office. There was a strong smell of liquorice, and his quick eyes picked out a row of tall jars of sweets.

He was so busy looking at them, he didn't notice that someone else had come in and was standing behind the counter, looking at them.

"Good day, Joe," she said, "...who's your friend?"

"Hello, Mrs Hughes," Joe replied. "He's Tim Oliver. He's come to stay at Crab Mill until the war's over."

"Welcome to Colemere Post Office, Tim!" said the Post-mistress. "So you're an evacuee! You're the first one I've met. Are your Mum and Dad staying with you?"

"No, they can't, " Tim replied. "My Dad's got to stay behind in Liverpool. He's doing important work for the war effort, and my Mum's got to stay to look after him and our house. There's only my sister, Shirley, and me...but they've promised to come and visit."

"Well," said Mrs Hughes smiling softly, "I think you're very brave to come and live so far from home...your sister, too. But I'm sure Joe's Mum and Dad will take good care of you, and..." she glanced along the counter at the jars "...I think I'll be seeing quite a lot of you, especially on Saturday mornings."

"What happens then?"

"You tell him, Joe!"

"That's when we spend our pocket money!"

"If Joe Everson wasn't one of my first customers on Saturday mornings, I'd think he must be ill!" the post-mistress laughed; then, as they were heading towards the door, she called out...

"See you next Saturday, Tim... and Joe, mind you look after your city friend. No getting him into trouble!"

Joe grinned. "I wonna', Mrs Hughes. Come on, Tim, I'll show you what else we'll be doin' on Saturday mornings."

He led the way round to a little shed-like building behind the Post Office. It had a doorway but no door, and inside there was a great heap of empty tin cans, all shapes and sizes, and some with their label still on – 'Baked Beans', 'Tomato Soup', 'Rice pudding'.

"What are they for?" Tim asked.

"It's the war effort," Joe pointed to a notice on the wall. It said

TURN YOUR CANS INTO CANONS!

"Everybody's supposed to bring their empty cans here and us lads come and bash 'em flat. Then a truck'll come around and take 'em to a factory to be made into tanks and planes and things."

He picked up a can with a label saying MUSHROOM SOUP, yelled "Achtung!" ('look out!') and hurled it across the room to crash into the wall.

Tim laughed. "I didn't know you could speak German, Joe!"

It was almost supper-time now and the tour was over. They left the tin-can mountain and ran back to the farm.

****

After breakfast the next Saturday, Mrs Everson gave out the pocket money, starting with Tim as the youngest.

"Here's your three-penny piece, Tim." She pronounced it 'thrippeny'. That's what your Dad said you should have, the same as Joe."

"Thank you, Mrs Everson," Tim said. "At home we call them 'joeys'."

The boys made straight for the Post Office. The door was always left open on Saturday mornings, because Mrs Hughes was fed up with the bell ringing every few seconds. The queue had already reached back to the door and Tim watched anxiously as the level of sweets in the jars dropped.

"Good morning, Tim," said the postmistress, when it was his turn, and he grinned. She had remembered his name.

"Now then, what can I get for you?"

He had already made a list of how much he could buy with his joey.

"A bar of Five Boys chocolate, an ounce of Everton mints, and an ounce of liquorice all-sorts, please."

Mrs Hughes weighed out the sweets, scooped them into a paper bag, and popped in a bar of chocolate.

"That'll be two-pence halfpenny." (She pronounced it tuppence haypenny). "Now…what great treat can I get you for your last haypenny? There's spearmint sticks and sherbert dabs…they're a haypenny each."

He thought hard, chose the spearmint, and handed over the joey.

Joe was next, and didn't take long choosing. He was particularly keen on aniseed balls, toffees and spearmint, but didn't seem interested in chocolate, which Tim thought was very surprising.

They walked down the path towards the tin can shed, which they could have found with their eyes closed. Inside two lads were kneeling down, bashing cans with hammers.

They looked up as Joe and Tim went in.

"This is Tim," said Joe.

"Hi, Tim!" they shouted back. They had seen him at school.

"Can we take over?" asked Joe.

"Have city lads got muscles?" one of them asked, with a grin.

They handed over their hammers, said 'cheerio', and left Joe and Tim with the mountain.

"It's not as easy as it looks," Joe said." The round ones are a bit tricky. If you don't hit them exactly right, they squirt away – like an orange pip. The best way is to hold them at one end…but watch your fingers!"

Tim did as he was told, and by the time they left the shed, his pile of flattened cans was almost as big as Joe's.

"That's nearly enough to make half a Spitfire, Joe," he laughed.

A letter from Crab Mill.

Dear Mum and Dad,

I quite like Crab Mill farm. Mr and Mrs Everson are very nice and Muriel and Joe are friendly. We have got jobs to do in the farm. I colect the eggs from the hen house in the top yard, and hunt for hidden nests. Some chickens are clever. They like to lay their eggs among the nettles. I think they know that humans don't like looking there. Joe showed me the field where Grandpa Dodd had his Scout camp and Mum helped. Our new school is very small, and the Headmistress is strikt. I don't think I will enjoy lessons. I hope you aren't lonely.

Please come and visit soon, and don't forget the Beanos.

Love, Tim

CHAPTER FOUR

FARMYARD STEEPLECHASE

Crab Mill Farm was laid out roughly in the shape of a rectangle, with two 'yards'. The main yard was in the centre, with the farm-house and garden on one side and the milking sheds on the other. There was a pump for fresh water, and a stone trough which was kept full for when Sheriff was thirsty. This was the 'lower' yard.

Another, very untidy, yard lay on higher ground behind the milking sheds. There was old machinery lying around; a tractor, which had once been the pride of the farmyard, but now lay there rusting, its wheels strangled by weeds and nettles; an ancient hay-cart with very flat tyres had been dumped there, and some old milk churns were standing in one corner looking quite sorry for themselves. In another corner stood the hen-house, which seemed to be the only reason anyone bothered to go there, so the residents could have the yard all to themselves, scratching around for worms and making the ground sticky. This was the 'upper' yard.

At both ends of the lower and upper yards there was a five-barred gate and that was what gave Geoff his bright idea.

Geoff Eccleston was the last evacuee to arrive at Crab Mill Farm. He came from Stockton Heath, a town situated halfway between Liverpool and Manchester. The ship canal for ocean-going merchant ships ran right through the town centre.

"That's why I came to Crab Mill," he explained. "My Dad says that if the bombers do come, the canal's bound to be a target."

He was nine, the same age as Muriel and Shirley, and very tall. Mrs Everson said that his legs 'seemed to go on forever'. He had a very loud voice and Joe said that when he laughed it was 'like crows quarrelling'.

The farmhouse was crowded now, and all the sleeping space was taken, so Mr Everson made a little room for him in the roof-space above Joe's bedroom, and Gerry, one of the farm workers, built a special ladder to reach it.

It was a lazy Saturday afternoon, and they were all in the upper yard trying to think of something interesting to do. The girls were perched on the old hay-cart swapping sweets, Joe was trying to do a balancing act on a rolling milk churn, and Tim was doing his best to make him fall off.

Geoff was bouncing up and down on the tractor seat, watching Joe and Tim, and imitating the crows.

Suddenly he yelled.

"Let's have a race! We could start at the pump," he waved an arm and pointed, "...over the gate into the orchard...round to the upper yard gate, over that and across the yard to the pond gate...over that," he stopped for a deep breath... "around the pond to the gate into the lower yard and back to the pump."

"A sort of steeplechase," said Joe.

"And it could be two laps," Tim piped up, "...just like the Grand National!"

FARMYARD STEEPLECHASE
– 2 LAPS –

Everyone agreed that it was a great idea, except Muriel who didn't like running of any kind and 'definitely not steeplechasing,' but said she would do her best.

"Now we need a few extra obstacles," said Geoff.

They tugged the hay-cart across the yard to make a tunnel, and stood the milk churns in a line. The boys fetched two hay-bales from the barn and laid them end-to-end to make a fence, which Geoff called 'a hurdle'; and that completed 'the course'. But Shirley was worried.

"The gates are really high, and Tim's legs are shorter than ours. It wouldn't be fair."

Tim was nodding. He had already measured himself against one of the gates. It did seem very high for someone of his size, and two laps meant there would be eight to climb over. Now he was sorry that he had mentioned the Grand National, and grateful to his big sister for sticking up for him.

There was a short discussion, and it was decided to give Tim a start of twenty paces and Joe a start of ten, to make it absolutely fair.

"O.K." said Geoff. "Everyone around to the pump."

They trooped down to the lower yard and did a few exercises... touching toes, swinging arms, jogging on the spot, and that kind of thing.

"Who's going to say 'GO'?" asked Muriel.

Nobody had thought about a 'starter'; but, at that moment, Mr Everson happened to be crossing the yard.

"Dad," Muriel called out, "can you spare a minute? We're going to have a steeplechase, and we need someone to be the starter."

The farmer looked quite pleased to be asked. He drew a line on the ground with his walking stick, took his floppy hat off and cleared his throat.

"Right then. Everyone line up!"

They stood with their toes up to the starting line, all except Joe and Tim, who had a bad case of butterflies in his stomach.

By now Mrs Everson and Bob and Gerry, the farm workers, had arrived to form a little crowd.

The starter lifted his hat.

"On your marks…get set…GO!"

He dropped his hat and the steeplechasers rushed towards the first gate. Tim got their first, as expected, but didn't bother climbing the five bars as you would climb a ladder. He had worked it out that, if you've got short legs, the quickest way over a five-barred gate is to put one foot on the middle bar, reach up to grab the top bar and put your tummy on it; then you reach down on the other side, grab a bar to steady yourself, throw your legs over and just drop to the ground, landing on your feet, if possible.

His plan worked well. He made a perfect two-point landing into the orchard, and was quickly into his running, up the slope to the gate into the upper yard. Joe was next, followed by Shirley. Geoff and Muriel discovered that there wasn't room on the top of the gate for two taller competitors at once, and got in each other's way in a tangle of legs. Geoff sportingly allowed Muriel to go first.

By this time Tim was already over gate number two into the upper yard and zig-zagging through the line of churns, scattering chickens in all directions. Ducking under the hay-cart was quite easy for someone of his size. He jumped the hurdle, but then made his big mistake. As he dropped down from gate number three, he glanced back through the bars of the gate to see how close the others were, even though his Dad had said 'NEVER LOOK BACK!' and forgetting that he was very close to the sticky edge of the pond.

The ducks had never seen anything like it before, and had retired to the middle of the pond to watch the little city boy skating around on the mud and poo. His feet were trying to go in different directions and he almost fell, but just managed to keep his balance, and headed for gate number four. He tumbled down into the lower yard and raced past the pump.

That was lap one completed. One lap to go.

Mrs Everson was clapping, Mr Everson waved his hat, and

Bob yelled "Go, tiny Tim!" Sherriff looked over his stable door, wondering what all the fuss was about, and even the cows in the top field paused to glance across, as Tim reached gate number five.

He was still well ahead, because the others were taking longer to get over the gates and under the cart, but, as he dropped down into the orchard for the second time, he took one more quick look back – he was glad his Dad wasn't watching – and got a shock. Geoff had overtaken Joe and Shirley with his gigantic strides and was gaining on him, perhaps only seven or eight strides away – he didn't waste time counting.

The gates seemed to be getting higher, and now he was really sorry that he had mentioned the Grand National. If it had been just one lap he would have won already!

The tacky ground of the upper yard felt like glue under his feet as he wormed his way through the churns for the second time and ducked under 'the tunnel'. It seemed much lower than on the first lap. The hurdle looked higher this time, too, and, as he launched himself into the air, his toe caught on the top and he crashed to the ground. But the butterflies wouldn't let him stop now, and in a second he was up and running again, knees covered with mud, clambering over gate seven, and skirting carefully around the mine-field which was the pond, to reach gate number eight.

It looked like a mountain. It WAS a mountain!

His legs were tired and bruised, and his tummy was sore, but he threw himself up, over and down into the lower yard. There was the pump and the finishing line, Mrs Everson clapping, Mr Everson throwing his hat in the air, and Bob and Gerry cheering.

He put his head back, gritted his teeth and was sprinting for the line when, OH NO! - out of the corner of his eye, he saw the long legs of Geoff striding past to reach the pump – the finishing post – first. Shirley just pipped Joe for third place, and Muriel was a brave last.

"Well run, Tim!" Geoff gasped. "I thought I'd never catch you."

Mr Everson rescued his dripping hat from the water trough. "Well run, Stockton Heath!" he shouted.

"And well run, little Liverpool!" Mrs Everson patted Tim on the back, and poor Tim sat on the ground and cried. His Dad had taught him how to be a good loser, but it wasn't easy. He had so nearly won.

Gerry rolled a milk churn over, pretending to catch his tears, and everyone laughed, even Tim.

"We canna' have a steeplechase without prizes!" said Mrs Everson. She hurried into the house, and came back with a handful of home-made toffee-apples. Bob and Gerry wheeled a trolley over to make a victory dais, and all five squeezed on to receive a prize, because, as Mr Everson explained in a little, impromptu speech...

"In the Olympic Games it says that the important thing is taking part, not winning."

Tim looked puzzled, as the farmer went on...

"And I think the Crab Mill Steeplechase was the most excitin' thing to happen in Colemere for years!"

****

These September days were hotter than usual. Joe's Mum said it was 'a real Indian summer', like summer over again, only 'with softer sunshine and longer shadows', and on Saturdays and Sundays, when they had done their jobs, the children took sandwiches, apples, damsons and home-made apple-juice onto the mere-field for games and swimming.

It was sandy at the edge of the mere, except for where the cows had been standing to keep cool; so if they didn't mind the cow-poo squeezing up between their toes, they could walk out a few yards to where it was deep enough to start swimming. Muriel, Joe and Geoff were strong swimmers and could easily reach the marker in the middle of the mere; but Tim could only dog-paddle a few frantic strokes, and stayed near the edge. Shirley hated tip-toeing over the poo, so she sat on the field reading her Girls Crystal.

One special day fell in September. It was Tim's eighth birthday on the 23rd, and he had dropped lots of hints in all directions, especially to his Mum.

"You don't think I would forget that date, do you, Tim?" She laughed. "Mums never forget birthdays!"

She came down by train for the day, and when Tim got home from school, she was waiting with an armful of presents from Grandparents, Aunts, Uncles and Godparents, including a 'Boys Book of Steam' to remind him of home, a pair of plimsolls - light, canvas 'running' shoes with rubber soles - specially requested by Tim 'for future steeplechasing', some adventure stories, a painting set, and a lot of sweets from thoughtful Auntie May, his Godmother, 'not to be eaten all at once!'

Mrs Everson had prepared a special tea, with a birthday cake and Tim's name on it, which was a great surprise. After all, he had only been at Crab Mill Farm for three weeks. The candles were blown out and the cake was cut. Then, it was time for Mum to catch the bus to the station, Tim, as the birthday boy, demanding the honour of carrying her bag to the bus stop, and Shirley holding on tight and only letting go as the door closed behind her.

The weeks went by and the trees around the mere began to change colour and shape as autumn came on. Mum and Dad took turns to visit at the week-ends, laden with comics, sweets and bits of news from home. If the weather was fine they would go for a picnic on the mere-field, and sit looking out over the peaceful water talking about the war which wasn't happening.

"The street's awfully quiet," Mum said, when she visited at half-term. "Billy's Mum says she would rather have him making a noise at home than being so far away in the country! She says you've all been away for seven weeks, and there's still no sign of any bombers; so it was probably a mistake to send you away, and you should all come home! But Dad and I think the government knows best, and it's safest for you to stay here."

Shirley didn't agree. Mum knew that she wasn't happy being away from home and they spent hours sitting together, holding hands and chatting quietly. But for Tim, living in the countryside was like being on a long holiday, making new friends and exploring new places in one huge 'park' without railings and ratty park-keepers. If it wasn't for school…

Monday morning always came around too soon. The Headmistress hardly ever smiled, and never at him. Luckily for Tim she spent most of her time with the smaller children, and gave the older ones exercises 'to get on with'. And he was still in his favourite place at the back of the class, where he could day-dream about football, trains and fighter-planes, until it was time to escape to the playground.

Most of the pupils liked the evacuees, especially the lively ones like Geoff and Tim. There were no P.E. lessons and, at play-times, Geoff showed them how to do hand-stands and cart wheels, and Tim took his football to school to show the smaller lads how to dribble and shoot. Shirley showed the girls how to do double-skipping with two ropes, generously supplied by Dad's factory.

Almost everyone wanted to be friends, but once or twice Tim noticed some of the other lads pointing at him and sniggering.

"Take no notice," said Joe.

CHAPTER FIVE

VILLAGE WARS

The Crab Mill boys reached the school gate one morning, to find a group of Lyneal boys blocking the way.

"Here's trouble!" muttered Joe.

Charlie Smythe was the toughest lad in the school. His Dad was the village blacksmith. His muscles reminded Tim of the huge mooring ropes at the factory, and Charlie had inherited them.

"We don't like evacuees," he snorted, pointing at Tim.

Tim was going to say 'Well, we don't like you either,' but Joe nudged him to keep quiet.

"City kids are sissies," Charlie went on, "and me and my gang want a fight."

His chums, Sid Simmons, a tall, rather skinny lad, Jerry Davies, who was half-hiding behind Charlie, and Reggie Fox who had reddish hair and a toothy grin, tried to look fierce, and joined in.

"Yeah...we want a fight!"

Tim gulped and tried to think of a good reason why they couldn't take up Charlie's challenge. Then he remembered his Dad saying that bullies don't like people standing up to them; so he looked Charlie in the eye, which wasn't easy, because Charlie had a slight squint.

"We'll have to talk about it," he said.

Tim, Joe and Geoff got in a huddle a few yards away.

"Trust Charlie to pick on the smallest one!" said Joe.

They all agreed that they would rather be friends.

"But if we don't fight, they'll say we're scared," Geoff whispered.

"And we dunna' have to attack 'em to show we anna' scared of 'em," added Joe, "we'll just defend ourselves."

"You're not an evacuee, Joe," said Tim. "You don't have to fight."

"But you're part of my family now, and families stick together."

"Thanks, Joe," said Tim, and walked back to Charlie.

"We're not looking for a fight, Charlie, but we're not scared of you and your gang either."

Charlie seemed surprised, and Sid, Jerry and Reggie looked disappointed.

"O.K," said Charlie. "Saturday mornin', halfway down The Drive at 10 o'clock…with sticks."

Tim gulped.

"We'll be there."

Joe, Tim and Geoff were on their way back down The Drive after school, chatting about Saturday's appointment with Charlie and his chums.

"We need one more fighter," said Tim.

They walked past the church and had almost reached the vicarage.

"What about James Pye?" said Joe. "I dunna' think he's scared of Charlie."

"Are vicar's sons allowed to fight?" asked Geoff.

"Well, we can soon find out!"

They trooped up the vicarage drive, and Joe knocked.

Mrs Pye, the vicar's wife, came to the door.

"Hello boys. This is a nice surprise, but I don't suppose you've come to volunteer to join the choir!"

Joe spoke up.

"No, Mrs Pye. We'd like to speak to James, please."

"Can I tell him what it's about?"

"Well, it's a bit of a secret at the moment."

"I see." She smiled. "Well, please wait here a moment."

She walked to the foot of the stairs and called out.

"James, come on down. There's a group of young gentlemen here to see you – on urgent business, I think."

There was a clattering of feet on the stairs, and the vicar's son appeared. James Pye was a bit older than Joe and Tim but younger than Geoff. He grinned when he saw the 'young gentlemen,' and his Mum left them to talk.

They told him about Charlie's challenge and what he had said about evacuees and 'city' boys

"We told him we'll fight, to show we're not scared," Tim explained, "...but we'll just defend ourselves".

"And we need one more fighter," said Joe. "Will you fight with us...if your Dad wouldn't mind?"

"Well, I'm not an evacuee. But I am a city boy; and I know my Dad doesn't like bullies. You should hear what he says about Mr Hitler! So I don't think he'll mind if I fight Charlie's lot with you."

"Well, that's our army," said Tim. "All we need now are our fighting sticks."

"There are lots of yew trees in the churchyard," said James. "They make the best bows out of yew, so they should make good fighting sticks, too. I'm sure no one'll notice if we cut a few branches."

He went to find a saw, then led the way across the church field and into the churchyard.

They worked out how long and thick a fighting stick should be – not too long or too heavy to swing, and not too short to stop attackers getting close. Then they picked out four straight yew branches, about an inch thick, and soon had one each. They spent a few minutes swinging them about, to get used to them.

"We need to guard our hands," said Geoff, "and I've got an idea. Come on!"

They followed him up to the village and into the tin can shed. Then they watched as he began rooting about, scattering cans everywhere, and when he stood up he was holding an oval-shaped can.

"That's what we need...pilchard tins!" he grinned. "Now we've got to find three more...so everybody get looking. If you can't see 'em, just sniff hard, and you'll find 'em!"

They started rummaging, and soon had four smelly pilchard tins, one each.

Back at Crab Mill they doused the tins under the pump and went to find Joe's Dad. Geoff told him about Charlie's challenge, and his idea for the hand-guards. The farmer looked at Tim and frowned.

"Oh, I dunna' think your Mum and Dad will be pleased to hear that you've been fightin', Tim."

"But I'm sure my Dad dunna' want me to be a sissie."

Mr Everson smiled. "Well, I think those Lyneal lads are in for a bit of a surprise!"

In the work-shop he took the lids off the cans and made a hole in each end with a heavy chisel and his hammer.

Then Geoff pushed his yew stick through the holes and bent the oval into a crescent shape. He slipped his hand under the crescent and gripped the stick.

"See...it makes a perfect hand-guard. Cavalry swords have them. My Uncle Arthur's got a real one. It's hanging on the landing wall upstairs, in case of burglars, I think!"

"Poor burglars!" Joe laughed.

All four hand-guards were soon fitted.

"Here, Joe," said Geoff. "Try and hit my hand."

Joe hit at Geoff's stick, and his stick slid down and came to a full stop at the hand-guard.

"It's brilliant!" Tim was excited. "Now all we need is to work out our tactics."

"There's four of us," said James. "Why don't we stand shoulder

to shoulder, in a sort of 'square', so we can be prepared, whatever direction they come from…like in 'Custer's Last Stand'…you know, when the army was surrounded by Redskins."

"But they were all wiped out, weren't they?" asked Joe.

"Yes! But that can't happen to us, can it?" James laughed, "not unless Charlie brings his Dad along!"

Tim volunteered to be at the front because, although he was the smallest, he had done the talking with Charlie, and, in any case, what with the special hand-guard and the thought of standing in a square, he was beginning to feel quite brave. They decided that Joe would be on his left side and Geoff on his right. James would complete the square, to guard their backs. Then they split into pairs, to practise for the battle.

****

Saturday came and the Crab Mill boys ate an extra bowl of porridge to build up their strength. Their first stop was the duck pond, where they smeared mud under their eyes, and on their cheeks and chins.

"It'll make us look a bit more fierce," said Joe, "and not so scared!"

At half-past nine they picked up their 'sabres' and cut across the mere-field to the vicarage.

James was waiting for them, and as they set off towards The Drive, they spotted the vicar standing at the study window. He gave a V-for-victory sign, which was as good as a prayer, because, although Tim had told Charlie they weren't scared, at that moment they were.

They headed up the Drive, their eyes focussed on the far end. The school clock said ten o'clock, but there was no sign of Charlie and his chums.

"D'you think they've forgotten?" asked Joe, hopefully.

"P'raps they're more scared than us," said Geoff. But at that moment the enemy came into sight, with Charlie in the lead. They could tell it was Charlie because he tended to strut, rather than walk.

His army plodded along behind him.

"Their sticks look too heavy," said James, "and they haven't got hand-guards."

"Try to keep in step," said Tim, "and look 'em in the eye."

The two armies marched slowly towards each other and halted on the wide verge. There was a gap of about twenty yards between them.

Sid and Jerry looked nervous. Reggie grinned toothily. Charlie scowled.

"So you've brought the vicar's son to fight us?" he sneered. "Well, you'd better start prayin', James Pye!"

James just grinned back, bravely.

Now Charlie glared at Tim, who remembered his Dad's advice and looked him in the eye, which Charlie didn't like.

He yelled "ATTACK!" and ran towards them, followed slowly by his army. The Colemere lads formed a square as they had practised, which seemed to confuse the attackers, because Reggie, Sid and Jerry pulled up, looking at each other as if they weren't sure what to do next. Charlie stopped too, realising that he was all by himself, only a few yards from the square and their sticks.

He turned and glared at his chums, again yelled "Attack!" and ran at the square, waving his stick wildly over his head. He aimed a blow at Tim who held his stick high across his chest and the bully's stick just bounced off. Charlie looked surprised, as if he had expected Tim's stick to shatter into little pieces at his first blow. He frowned and dropped back a few steps.

His army wasn't having much success either. James and Joe noticed that Sid and Jerry weren't as keen on fighting as their leader. Sid was making grunting sounds and just glaring at James, and Jerry was taking a long time tying a shoe lace. The only fighting was between Geoff and Reggie who had dropped their sticks and were wrestling on the ground.

Now Charlie came back on the attack. His stick caught Tim's, but slid down and stopped at the hand-guard. Tim grinned, and brought his stick down hard on the bully's arm. His face turned red and he dropped back again, rubbing his arm and frowning. This skinny city lad was tougher than he looked.

Then he thought he would try his luck fighting Joe. But that was a great mistake because, although Joe wasn't very tall, he was very strong, as farmer's sons usually are, and when the bully rushed at him with his head down, Joe was ready for him. He stepped forward quickly, and before Charlie could even raise his heavy stick, he whacked him hard on his hand, making him drop it.

That was enough for Charlie. He picked up his stick, shouted "RETREAT!" and ran back up The Drive followed quickly by his army.

"They're beaten!" shouted Joe. "Should we go after 'em?"

"No... let 'em go," said Tim. "Now they know that city kids can stick up for themselves."

The school clock showed 10.22. It had been a very short battle. 'More like a skirmish', Uncle Arthur would have said, but 'a very decisive one'!

"General Custer would've been proud of us," said James, as they marched smartly back home.

At school on Monday morning, Charlie was standing in the playground with his arm in a sling, relating how he and his gang had been ambushed by 'at least ten evacuees' and would have won a great victory 'if they hadn't run away'. But nobody believed him.

****

Meanwhile, the Nazi bully had overrun Poland, and his bombers had demolished Warsaw, the beautiful capital city. Would England and London be their next stop? Everyone wondered and waited...and waited, as the weeks passed by with no sign of any bombers.

Tim's Dad said that bullies respect people who stand up to them. So perhaps Herr Hitler had decided to leave Britain alone, and perhaps Billy's Mum was right after all.

The evacuees might as well come home.

CHAPTER SIX

HOME AGAIN

A few days after the battle with Charlie, Geoff's Mum and Dad arrived at Crab Mill Farm.

"It was a false alarm," said his Dad. "The bombers didn't turn up after all, so we've come to take him home."

Some of the other evacuees went home, too. Tim thought the Headmistress would be pleased, and at last he had a desk to himself.

Then a letter came to say that, as the danger had gone away, Mum would be coming to take them back to Liverpool. Tim had almost forgotten what home was like, and wasn't sure that he wanted to leave. But Shirley started to pack straight away.

Mrs Oliver came down the next Saturday with a plant in a pot for Mrs Everson and a fountain pen each for Muriel and Joe. She thanked them for making space in their bedrooms and for being such good friends.

Muriel and Joe said it had been 'great fun'.

"And a lot more exciting than usual!" said Joe.

"It's been a pleasure having them," said Mrs Everson, handing over a dozen new-laid eggs, and not forgetting to mention that Tim had 'searched high and low' to find them.

"No nest is safe when Tim Oliver is on the prowl!"

The egg-collector said he would 'definitely' be coming back to Crab Mill in the summer holidays, and Shirley and Muriel promised to write.

Then, after 'goodbyes' the evacuees were heading back home.

The Welbeck Avenue folk had heard that the Oliver kids were coming home, and when the Morris pulled up outside number 6, front doors opened and they came out to wave.

"Welcome home, country kids!"

But Shirley didn't feel at all like a 'country kid'.

"I'm a city kid!" she said. "Crab Mill Farm was very nice, but this is my home, and Hitler's bombers will have to knock it flat to change that!"

Mrs Thompson came across to say that Billy was staying with the school in Wales until the Easter holidays. She wasn't pleased.

"I don't understand why they haven't come home, too!"

To the evacuees the Avenue looked exactly the same as when they went away, except for the windows, which were criss-crossed with sticky tape.

"That's to stop glass flying everywhere if a bomb explodes nearby," Mum explained.

The neighbours retreated and the Olivers went indoors. A cake on the table said WELCOME HOME! in pink and blue icing.

Shirley noticed the new, dark curtains.

"They're so gloomy!"

"It's for the black-out," Mum explained. "When it's dark, there mustn't be the smallest chink to let light out. Otherwise an enemy pilot might spot it and think he'd reached his target. We hope they'll never come, but we must do the black-out every night just in case, or we'd get into serious trouble from the wardens!"

"Who are they?" asked Tim.

"They're a kind of unofficial policeman with a tin hat and a loud, bossy voice. They're always on the look-out after dark."

At that moment Dad came in and swooped on them for a big hug. Then they sat around the table enjoying the cake.

"Is the war over, Dad?" asked Tim, in between mouthfuls.

"No, Tim, it isn't," he shook his head. "Adolf Hitler says he doesn't want to fight Britain, and he'll leave us alone if we make peace. But we've told him that we'll never make peace with the Nazis - that's his government - and we know what has happened to poor Poland. So we must be prepared. Come on...I'll show you our air-raid shelter."

They followed him through the kitchen and across the yard. The back alley had almost disappeared, and instead of the space where the boys used to play cricket, there was a very odd-looking building. It was built of brick, and sandwiched between the walls on either side of the lane. The flat roof was just a very thick layer of concrete and the solid metal door was guarded by a brick wall.

Dad led the way in.

Straightaway Tim wrinkled his nose at the bitter smell of concrete. Narrow slits in the walls, filled with glass, allowed a tiny amount of daylight in, and they could pick out the shape of bunk-beds, benches and old, rickety card tables. Otherwise it was just an empty space, and the evacuees were not impressed.

Mum put on a brave smile.

"I know it's not much like home, but, if we do have to spend the night here, you'll be surprised how comfy we'll make it."

Tim was puzzled.

"But if the danger's gone away, why do we need all the sticky tape and gloomy curtains...and this smelly shelter?"

"It's just a precaution, Tim."

It was almost dark when they got back to number 6, and time to do the black-out. Tim's bedroom was at the back of the house and he was puzzled again.

"Why do I have to black-out my windows? Hardly anyone looks at the back of houses."

Dad laughed.

"That doesn't mean the German pilots wouldn't look at them, Tim. They're trained to pick out the smallest beam of light wherever it comes from! So you'd better get covering!"

****

The next morning Tim was in his usual place on the end wall to watch the 'Scot' go by. It was right on time, as usual, but not his favourite driver. Tim guessed that he had probably been called up to fight against the 'nasties'. The new one seemed a lot older, and didn't even look his way.

Tim was hoping that the London, Midland and Scottish railways had brought some new engines and rolling-stock into service while he had been away, but he was out of luck. There was nothing new to be seen.

Dad explained. "The locomotive factories are making tanks and armoured cars now, and the car factories are turning out aeroplanes!"

The Christmas holidays had already started, and Tim thought he would put up with the smell and make a den in the shelter. He asked if he and Shirley could reserve a double bunk-bed for themselves, and Mum said they could, as there were enough for all the children. Then he asked Shirley if he could have the top bunk.

"Yes, you can, Tim," she said, "just as long as you promise to stay still, and don't make it wobble about!"

He put his name on the side, piled some old Beanos into a cardboard box and hoisted it onto his bunk.

Now he was ready for the bombers.

Most of the evacuees were still away, so the Avenue was quiet, except when Art came around. The words on the side of his cart said 'Arthur Smethurst, dealer in rags and bones.' Tim had always wondered what kind of bones he dealt in, and what use they could be; but nobody seemed to know. It was all a bit spooky.

A small union jack - Art's contribution to the war-effort - flew from the back of the cart, which was drawn by a grey pony called Sybil, after a famous aunt who had served with the Votes for Women campaigners. She had been arrested at the Pier Head for leaping aboard the Mersey Pilot boat waving a banner, and refusing to get off.

The cart had a trumpet-like horn with a rubber ball on the end, which Art squeezed every now and then to let people know he'd arrived. It wasn't very tuneful. In fact Tim said it sounded like a Crab Mill cow with a bad cough; and Art's voice sounded just like the horn. But he was a friendly chap, and Tim wanted to give him some business.

Before the war he used to pester his Mum to look out an old jumper or something which she hardly ever wore, and Tim, as the 'middle man', would get a reward...some cigarette cards, or marbles or a balsa-wood aeroplane kit. Now he was the only kid in the Avenue apart from the little ones at number 16, and they were too young to be in the rag-and-bone trade; and Shirley, who hated the sound of the horn and the voice, always stayed indoors while her brother carried on his private enterprise. So he could have his pick of the rewards. But now the government was telling everyone to keep their old clothes, so business was bad, and Art and his eager assistant often went empty-handed.

With no Billy and Sid and Ken around, Tim spent the time in his new den reading his Beanos, or practising shooting his football against the end wall; or, to keep warm in the chilly December wind, he ran up and down the street for hours with his whip and top. It didn't matter if the string wore out. There was enough at the factory to keep him whipping for years.

****

On Christmas Day the family went to church. They sang '*Hark the herald angels sing*' and the vicar's sermon was about 'Peace on earth and mercy mild'.

"This very morning, people all over Germany will be celebrating the birth of Jesus, 'the Prince of Peace', while their armies are preparing for war! And how much mercy have they shown to Poland? But that's what can happen when a nation has bad leaders."

"Aren't there any good leaders in Germany, Dad?" They were on their way home and Shirley had been thinking hard. "What about the teachers and doctors and businessmen like you. Can't they persuade the Nazis to be peaceful and merciful?"

"Well Shirley, there are many good people there who don't agree with Hitler, and do speak out; but they risk being sent to prison. Even the newspapers daren't tell the truth. They have to print what they're told. They praise Hitler and say how he really wants peace, and that it's us who want war."

The grandparents came to lunch and it was the happiest Christmas ever. The danger had gone away and the evacuees had come home. Shirley had been busy hanging up little paper lanterns, and Tim had made enough paper-chains to decorate most of the house, plus one or two spares for the shelter, 'in case there's an air-raid at Christmas'.

After lunch everyone squeezed into the front room to exchange presents. Mum and Dad gave Tim a model-kit of the new Spitfire fighter-plane, and he was sitting on the floor checking that all the parts were there, when Dad turned the wireless on. The chattering stopped, and for the first time in his life, Tim heard the voice of the King.

He thought it sounded rather quiet for a King, and everyone listened carefully as he spoke about the dark shadow which was falling over the world because of the Nazis.

"Don't be afraid," he said, and quoted some famous words: 'Go out into the darkness and put your hand into the hand of God. That shall be to you better than light and safer than a known way'."

That cheered everyone up and they sat around sipping tea, munching mince-pies and chatting about the King's message and the rationing. But when Grandma Oliver started on her favourite topic – 'ten different ways of making an ordinary potato taste delicious', Tim slipped away to his bedroom to start assembling his Spitfire.

He spent the rest of the holidays finishing and painting it with its grey/green camouflage and the Royal Air Force logo – blue and white rings with a red centre. Then Dad helped him to hang it from the ceiling over his bed, and he could lie on his back imagining himself in the cockpit, diving out of the sun, all eight canons blazing away, and shooting half a dozen enemy bombers down in flames.

The holidays ended too soon. They always did for Tim, and it was back to school. The sticky tape was everywhere, so the classrooms seemed gloomier than ever. But some of the other evacuees were trickling back now, and there were enough lads for football.

Tim's hero was Dixie Dean, the famous Everton centre-forward, and he was hoping to be picked to play for the Dovedale Road School Under 9s against Bridge Road School. The day before the game, the team was pinned up on the notice board. His name was there – Tim Oliver OR - and the teacher handed him his school shirt with the number seven - for outside right - on the back. It had yellow and green halves and was very faded, because so many keen mums had washed it; but he didn't mind that. To Tim it was as good as an England shirt, and he was so excited he ran all the way home, across Penny Lane and along Crawford Avenue, waving it over his head.

Dovedale Road won the match 3-1. The teacher said that Tim hadn't forgotten how to dribble while he was away in the country, and now he could shoot with both feet, which pleased his Dad.

CHAPTER SEVEN

ENEMY AT THE GATES

Just before the Easter holidays Mrs Thompson knocked at number 6 to say that Billy was coming home and to ask if Tim would like to go and meet him off the train. He didn't need to be asked twice.

Wavertree Station was only three minutes away. It was raised high up above the road, level with the embankment, and he ran ahead up the three flights of stairs, two steps at a time, to the platform.

A large crowd of mums and a few dads had assembled, and when the train puffed into sight, with heads and arms sticking out of every window, there was a loud cheer. It had hardly screeched to a halt, in a great cloud of steam, before doors flew open and evacuees spilled out onto the platform as fast as if someone had emptied a bag of snakes into the carriages.

The teachers got off last, and Mrs Thompson caught sight of Mr Donaldson, Billy's teacher, looking very hot and glad to have arrived. Then she spotted Billy and waved. He pushed his way through the crush, and Tim stood back waiting, while Mrs Thompson crushed Billy in a long hug.

When it was his turn he patted Billy on the back.

"Hi, Billy. Welcome home!" he said, as if he hadn't been away at all himself.

Then he spotted Sid and Ken who were being hugged themselves, and they all agreed to meet up 'on the wall' the next morning.

Tim was already in position when the others scrambled up alongside. He and Billy had brought their train-spotters' gear with them in case something special went by. Ken and Sid weren't keen spotters, but wanted to know what Tim had been doing on the farm while they were in Wales.

They waited until the 'Scot' had thundered past.

Then Billy started.

"The day after you went to the Farm, the Headmaster told us in assembly that we were being evacuated to a friendly town in North Wales, called Wrexham. He said we would be staying with families and he wanted us to be on our best behaviour – 'good ambassadors for Dovedale Road School!'"

"It was a real crush at the station. The grown-ups were crying more than the kids. Mr Donaldson was going with us. He told the Mums not to worry, and he would make sure we would write and tell them where we were staying."

Sid butted in. "Danny Kelly sat on the platform and said he wasn't going. His Mum didn't know what to do. Then Kenny Webster said Danny could be in the football team if he got on the train; so he cheered up and got on."

Ken took up the story. "We leaned out of the windows to wave, and Frank Wilson nearly fell out! We sang 'Ten green bottles' and 'Old McDonald'".

"When we got to Wrexham we went into a big hall with tables loaded with butties and cakes and pop. A jolly man with a gold chain made a speech…I think he was the Lord Mayor."

'Girls and boys from Liverpool, welcome to WrexHAM,'– that's how he pronounced it. Some ladies were there and we wondered which one would be looking after us. We had to stand up when our name was called."

"I was almost the last," said Billy, "'cos my name starts with a 'T', and when they came to me, they said 'Billy Thompson will stay with Mrs Davies at 23, Oswestry Road'. I stood up, and a lady came over and said 'Hello, Billy, I'm Mrs Davies. Would you like to stay with me and my family?'"

"I said 'Yes, please,' and she laughed. Then we went to her house. Mr Davies works in a quarry…he's got a bad chest and coughs a lot. They've got two children, called Bronwen and Owen, and they said I was one of the family. I had my own bedroom, and Mrs Davies always divided everything up equally. "

He stopped speaking as a goods train clattered past.

"The next day I went with Bronwen and Owen to their school. All our class was there and we had our own classroom, with Mr Donaldson to teach us. It was like being back at Dovedale. The headmaster said he hoped we played rugby, 'cos Welsh lads don't play footie much. We played rugby a lot, even in the rain. You get much muddier than in footie, but it's fun, specially if you're in the scrum!"

"I was with an old lady called Mrs Morgan," said Sid. "She lives close to the market. She used to be a teacher. I could tell that, 'cos she kept wagging her finger and telling me off for not tidying my bedroom up. She tried to teach me to speak Welsh and I learnt a few words. 'Nos da' is 'good night' and 'Bendigedig' means 'God bless'. She was nice...but I really missed my Mum."

"Me too," said Ken. "Mrs Llewellyn, who I stayed with, was a very happy lady. She was always singing...it was usually in Welsh, and a lot of hymns, I think. She said everybody sings in Wales. Sometimes Mr Llewellyn joined in, but he wasn't very good, so I went to my room and read my Dandy. They were kind though... I think they felt sorry for us."

"Every Saturday the town was full of Mums and Dads from Liverpool," said Sid, "and I think the shops ran out of sweets. Then last week, Mr Donaldson told us that we were going home because the bombers hadn't come."

"We all cheered," said Billy, 'cos we wanted to be back at home...but it was sad, really, saying 'bye-bye'."

Then it was Tim's turn to talk about Crab Mill Farm and Joe, and his jobs for the 'war-effort' – tin can bashing and outsmarting the clever chickens. He described the mere and old Sam, the friendly Postmistress and the unfriendly Headmistress. He told the story of the battle with Charlie and his chums, and when he described the steeplechase and skating about on the duck-poo, Sid laughed so much, he nearly fell off the wall.

Now, in the park, it was cricket instead of football. The iron railings and gates had been taken away for the war effort, and there was no closing-time, because there were no gates to close. So the boys could stay as long as they liked and annoy the park-keeper. Life was more fun than ever, and the war, if there was one, seemed a long way away. It was May 1940.

****

Then soon after the start of the summer term, there was grim news on the wireless at number 6.

The Nazi armies were on the move again. They had already overrun Norway, Denmark, and Holland and were heading with frightening speed across Belgium towards France. The poster outside the newspaper kiosk by the station, where Tim bought his Beano, carried just one word in big letters...

'BLITZKRIEG!'

"What does it mean, Dad?" asked Tim.

"Something like 'lightning strike', Tim. They attack without warning and very quickly, so people aren't prepared."

There was worse news to come. A British army had been sent to try to stop the German advance, but had been forced to retreat, and was trapped between the German army and the English Channel.

The poster at the kiosk said 'TRAPPED!' and the Echo newspaper told the story.

'The British troops are stranded on the beaches near the port of Dunkirk at the mercy of the German dive-bombers, and there aren't enough ships to take them to safety.'

"They won't just be left there, will they, Dad?" Shirley asked.

"Of course not, Shirley! Mr Churchill, the new Prime Minister,

has sent out an urgent message asking everyone who has a boat that's big enough, to sail to Dunkirk and rescue them."

"The dive-bombers wouldn't attack them, would they, Dad?" asked Tim. "That wouldn't be fair, would it, when they can't defend themselves?"

"Well, Tim, this enemy doesn't always play by the rules. They'll do anything to stop our army getting away, so any kind of boat trying to take them off the beaches will be a target. It's going to be a dangerous mission."

"D'you think old Sam's punts could help? They can hold at least ten people, as long as they all sit still." Tim was imagining Joe and himself sailing to the rescue with Sam in charge. It seemed a shame to think of the punts just lying there in the boathouse, when they could be out saving soldiers.

Dad smiled

"Sam's punts might be alright if the Channel was as calm as the mere, Tim; but it can be very rough, so I don't think they would get very far."

It was a dangerous mission, as Dad said it would be. But on the wireless the next evening, they heard that hundreds of little boats, all shapes and sizes – sailing boats, barges, and pleasure boats – had set out for France, and were 'at that very moment' rescuing the troops. Some of the brave skippers went back again and again; some lost their boats, and some lost their lives.

Then, at last, the news came through that most of the army had been brought back home safely and would live to fight another day.

The poster said… MIRACLE!

But then there was more bad news. France had surrendered and the mighty German army stomped up the Champs Elysees in the French capital.

Now Britain was alone against the Nazis, and only the Channel lay between their bomber-bases in France and the south of England. "That's about six minutes flying time," Dad muttered grimly. "Too close for comfort!"

****

One morning, just before the summer holidays, the Headmaster came into assembly with two prefects, each carrying a small cardboard box.

"Girls and boys," he began, "Hitler is gobbling up his neighbours one after another, and I fear he won't leave our little island alone. It may not be long before his bombers are flying across the English Channel, even as far as our city, and we must be prepared. We have our air-raid shelters, but they won't protect us from a gas attack, so we must all have a gas-mask."

He turned to the prefects. "Cynthia and Gerald have brought theirs into assembly, and they will show us how easy it is to put them on."

Cynthia smiled sweetly and confidently, as if she was used to demonstrating how to put a gas-mask on. Gerald looked a bit uncertain.

They opened their boxes and each took out something that looked like motor-cycle goggles with a large, round nose attached and an elastic band at the back. Cynthia worked quickly, putting her chin into the round 'nose' end, then pulling the elastic band over her head. The mask was soon in place and she was breathing deeply, and smiling at the audience, although they didn't know it because her face was almost invisible.

Gerald was having a struggle getting the elastic band in position behind his ears which were unusually large; but with a little help from the Headmaster he finally had his mask in place.

"There now," said the Head, smiling, "…you see how quickly it can be put on, although it might take some of us a little longer than others." Gerald turned pink but, luckily, his face was also hidden from the audience, so nobody could tell.

Back in the classroom there was a gas-mask on each desk and everyone had a lot of fun trying to recognise the others.

Tommy Dalton noticed that if he breathed out hard, the window misted over, so he couldn't see out and the others couldn't see in.

Mr Donaldson put his mask on last.

Alex McMinn laughed. "He looks better with his mask on!"

"How will we know when to put our mask on, sir?" asked Grace Vernon.

"There will be a special siren, Grace…just one long note, so it's important to be able to tell the difference."

"What happens if it's tea-time and we're hungry?" asked Lily Rogers, who had a very large appetite.

"We'll just have to wait for the air-raid to end, won't we, Lily?" He smiled.

"And all of you…remember to keep your gas-mask ready at all times, whether there's a raid or not!"

So that evening at 6, Welbeck Avenue, four little boxes sat on a shelf at the front door, next to Dad's fire-watcher's helmet, ready for action.

CHAPTER EIGHT

BLITZ AND BOMBS

The summer holidays came at last and the four pals spent most of the time playing cricket in the park or 'cops and robbers' in the back alleys. The gloomy air-raid shelters made great hiding places and the sound of pretend machine-gun fire echoed around the empty spaces, so their mums knew where they were. They had already forgotten about the headmaster's solemn warning.

A few days before the end of the holidays, Billy and Tim decided to check out the 'Cast Iron' shore, which was only a twenty minutes' bus-ride away. The 'Casie' wasn't the nicest beach in the world. In fact it wasn't really a beach – just a long stretch of muddy shoreline on the north side of the river Mersey. Tim's Mum said it was 'ugly', like its name, and 'bleak', and she couldn't understand why they bothered going.

Before the war they used to scavenge among the flotsam and jetsam washed up by the tide, and watch the funny little 'banana' boats jostling with cargo ships on the way to and from the ship canal. But there were no banana boats now, and the shore was littered with boring concrete blocks and rolls of barbed wire keeping nosey schoolboys out and the enemy from getting in. So there wasn't much to do.

They perched themselves on an old log which had been dumped there one particularly high tide, munching their sandwiches and chatting about unpleasant things like the war and going back to school, and pleasant things such as who would be in the under 10s football team when the new season started.

"My Mum says everything's going to be rationed soon," said

Billy, "...even sweets."

"SWEETS!" Tim pulled a face. "That's not fair!"

They sat contemplating the bad news, and tossing a crust or two to a brave sea-gull which had ventured over to the log in the hope of a hand-out.

"My Mum says we can get into trouble for giving crusts to the birds, now it's wartime," said Tim. "She says we're not supposed to waste anything, so they'll have to look after themselves. But I think that's a bit cruel. It's not their fault there's a war on!"

Billy nodded thoughtfully, and they munched on.

Through the barbed wire they spotted a brand new motor torpedo boat, Ensign flying proudly from the stern, and guns at the ready, making big bow-waves as it hurried past.

When they looked towards the mouth of the river they could easily pick out the strange 'Liver Birds' perched high up on the city sky-line - giant imitation cormorants with long, spindly legs and wide-spread wings. Higher still were the even-stranger wartime sky-creatures - huge, flabby barrage-balloons swinging about lazily on their cables, massive, elephant-like 'ears' flapping in the wind as if listening out for the sound of approaching bombers.

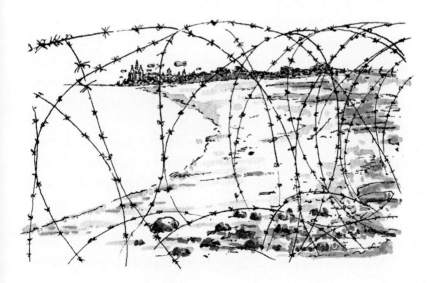

They finished their sandwiches and headed for the bus stop, leaving the concrete and barbed wire to the hungry seagulls.

Now, in the sky over the South of England, Royal Air Force fighter-squadrons were already locked in great battles with swarms of enemy bombers and their fighter escorts. The Headmaster was right. Hitler wasn't leaving Britain alone. He had given his bombers the order to attack.

Suddenly the war seemed much closer, and every night Tim checked his black-out carefully.

****

Then one evening, soon after dark, the eerie wailing sound of a siren filled the air over Welbeck Avenue. It started quietly, then got louder, rising and falling. Tim was fast asleep after a hard day's cricket, and didn't hear it; but Shirley was still awake.

She ran into his room and shook him.

"Tim, wake up!"

He didn't move. She shook him again.

"WAKE UP, Tim. It's an air raid!"

He opened his eyes, heard the siren and jumped out of bed just as Dad came upstairs.

"The bombers will be here in about fifteen minutes." He tried to speak calmly. "Don't be afraid. Just put your dressing-gowns on, and Mum will take you to the shelter...and don't forget your gas-masks!"

He hugged them, then hurried downstairs, picked up his helmet and gas-mask and went to report to his fire-watchers' post. Shirley glanced after him anxiously. Fire-watchers had no air-raid shelters to hide in.

Mum had packed some drinks and biscuits, and led the way through the inky darkness into the back alley. Search-lights were already criss-crossing the sky, ready to pick out the bombers for the anti-aircraft gunners to shoot at. Shirley was very quiet and kept looking up. Tim was wide awake now, and excited.

As they reached the shelter the wailing died away.

Everyone from the Olivers' side of the street had squeezed in, except Mrs Ferguson from number 12, who said she wasn't going to leave Henry, her parrot, alone in the house 'with nasty bombs exploding all around him,' ...and anyway, she couldn't stand the horrid smell. But when Mrs Impitt from number 8 explained that, 'as the grandma of the street', she would be needed to keep everybody's spirits up, she changed her mind. The rules said that pet birds were not allowed in the shelters, so Henry, who was known to be quite high-spirited and to use rude words at times, was left behind in the front room with a blanket over his cage and a record of hymns playing in the background 'to keep him cheerful'. She brought Charles, her large cat, instead.

Shirley and Tim settled down on their bunks. The two children from number 16 also had bunks. Everyone else tried to make themselves comfortable on benches, which wasn't easy, and deck-chairs. Tim was disappointed that Billy's side of the street had its own shelter, so they couldn't be together to share the excitement.

Mrs Jones from number 2 was already busy making cups of tea, and her daughter, Gladys, carried them around on a tray with some digestive biscuits. People spoke in whispers, and some tried to read a book or newspaper. Mum sat with Shirley on the lower bunk, talking quietly. Tim concentrated on his Beanos, but with one ear open for the sound of bombers.

The minutes ticked away and he was getting impatient. Were they coming, or weren't they?

Then, in the quietness, they heard the sound that no one, except Tim, wanted to hear – the sinister brm-brm-brm-brm of Dornier bomber engines, as a wave of planes passed overhead, and soon afterwards the crunching sound of distant explosions, mingled with the regular boom-boom-boom-boom of Anti-Aircraft guns.

"They've found the docks," said Mr Impitt.

Another wave flew over, and some of the explosions sounded much nearer. Mr Impitt, who seemed to be an expert on bombing, continued his commentary.

"They were a bit close! Perhaps they're aiming for the railway."

Tim frowned and hoped he was wrong.

There was no whispering now. Just an anxious silence, except for Mrs Ferguson who seemed to have got used to the smell already, and was reading Psalm 23 out loud from a well-worn Bible. "The Lord is my shepherd…even when I walk through the valley of the shadow of death…"

Tim hadn't thought of an air-raid in that way.

The mother of the two small children was singing quietly to them, and Shirley held tight to her Mum. Tim was a bit scared too, now, but he wasn't going to let it show. Instead, he was thinking about bombs and shrapnel – the bits which fly everywhere when a bomb explodes. Where did they fly, and, even more importantly, where did they land? He was sure there must be some lying around in the street, just waiting to be picked up. He had brought an empty Meccano box with him, in case he was lucky enough to find some; but people weren't supposed to leave the shelter while there was a raid on.

'There can't be any harm in just looking in our street,' he said to himself. 'It'll be too late in the morning. The bin men'll be coming around to brush up the shrapnel and take it to the dump, and that would be a terrible waste.'

His Mum was busy chatting to Mrs Jones and he took his chance. Tucking the box under his dressing gown, he slipped out into the darkness, ran to the end of the lane and turned into Welbeck Avenue. Search-lights were still sweeping the sky to chase away any raider that might still be hanging about, and a fire-engine rushed past the end of the Avenue, bell clanging furiously.

He had already decided that the best place to hunt for shrapnel would be in a gutter or against a wall - any place where a flying object couldn't fly any further. His eyes were soon used to the darkness and, as he reached the end wall they picked out a shiny object lying right under his favourite train-spotting perch.

It was shaped like a spinning top and he guessed that it must be the nose of a bomb. He stooped down to check that it wasn't hot, glancing over his shoulder, like a gold prospector afraid his claim might be 'jumped'. Then he picked it up quickly, took the lid off his box and dropped it in.

'Just wait 'til the lads see this,' he grinned.

Then he saw a figure wearing a helmet and arm-band with a big 'W' on it, striding quickly towards him through the darkness. Tim hadn't met an Air Raid Warden before, but guessed that this must be one.

The grin vanished.

"What are you doing here?" The warden snapped.

Tim started to explain, but he was cut short.

"You get back to your shelter, my lad, and be quick about it!"

Tim turned and ran back the way he had come, around the end of the terrace and into the shelter.

Inside, the talking stopped and everyone seemed to be looking at him. His Mum was surrounded by a little group of ladies looking very concerned, and he could tell that she had been crying. He hated it when she cried, especially when it was his fault. Shirley was sitting on her bunk, pretending to read. Mum made her way between the deckchairs and card tables to where he was standing by the door, biting his lip.

"Where have you been, Timothy?" She always called him that when she was upset or angry with him, and she didn't wait for an answer.

"How dare you leave the shelter…and what have you got in that box?"

"Erm…" said Tim.

"Show me!" she said, and slowly he took the lid off.

The nose-cone looked shinier and more impressive than ever,

even in the dim light.

"Whatever is it?" she demanded.

"It's shrapnel, Mum – part of a bomb," Tim replied quite proudly, holding it out for her – and anyone else who might be interested – to have a close look.

"And where did you find it?"

"In the street, Mum."

The shelter had gone even quieter now. Everyone knew that 'young Tim' was in serious trouble. Shirley was trying not to giggle.

His Mum wiped her eyes.

"You were very foolish to go out into the street during an air-raid...you might have been killed. Just wait 'til your father comes home."

Tim gulped.

Mum continued.

"As a punishment you may not have your Beano for two weeks... and you may not keep your silly bit of bomb!"

She held out her hand.

Tim was stunned. Losing his comics was bad enough, but he hated giving up his shrapnel. It wasn't silly. In fact, at that moment it was his proudest possession, he reckoned, even more than his

football; and he knew that, if he told the other lads that he'd found 'the actual nose of a bomb' they would want to see it. He handed over the box, then climbed up onto his bunk, nibbled a digestive, and thought about his bad luck.

Just then the all-clear siren sounded. Everyone picked up their bits and pieces and filed out into the darkness. Tim went straight to bed before Dad got home.

The next day was Saturday, and he was determined to get up early for some legal souvenir hunting; but, after his late night, he had over-slept, and when he ran out into the Avenue, it seemed to be full of kids clutching boxes and bags, examining every inch of the gutters and gardens. There were a few dads there too, as keen as the kids. He was too late.

Billy was there, but hadn't had any luck. Tim told him about his night-time adventure and 'amazing find', and he pretended to be very impressed, but said he 'would like to see it some time'.

One of the girls had found a twisted metal cylinder which smelt like a burnt-out firework. A Dad said that it was probably an incendiary bomb.

"At least that one didn't start any fires!" he added.

Some of the others had picked up scraps of black metal which weren't very exciting, and one by one they gave up the search and left the street to the bin men.

When Tim got home, his Dad was waiting for him. He was holding the nose-cone.

"Have you any idea, Tim, how fast this would be moving when the bomb exploded... and what would happen if someone got in its way?"

There was no answer.

"Well, I'll tell you. If it had been you, your Mum and I would be arranging a funeral today." He stopped speaking for a few moments, to let the idea sink in.

"Do you realise what a dangerous thing you did, leaving the shelter like that?"

Still there was no answer.

"Your mother was desperate, not knowing where you had gone."

By now Tim wasn't trying to hide his feelings, and tears were running down his cheeks.

"Now you can go to your bedroom and think about what has happened."

It was nearly lunch-time when Tim went downstairs to find Mum.

"I'm very sorry I left the shelter, Mum," he began. "I didn't understand how dangerous it was".

She could see that he had been crying and didn't say a word. She just put her arms around him. And that was the end of that – almost.

CHAPTER NINE

A DUD

'This is the BBC Home Service and here is the news...'

Shirley put down her Girls' Crystal and listened.

'Last night the Liverpool docks were bombed and badly damaged.'

"Perhaps they've done all the damage they wanted to do, and won't bother coming back, Dad."

"We must hope so, Shirley."

But, as it got dark, the sirens wailed again.

The Olivers were ready this time, and almost first into the shelter. Tim climbed onto his bunk and buried his head in Beanos, pretending not to notice as people glanced up at him, wondering what had happened when his Dad got home the previous night. Gladys was feeling sorry for him, and pressed some extra biscuits into his hand.

Everyone was used to the shelter now, and there was lots of activity. Shirley had brought LUDO and SNAKES & LADDERS to try to persuade the small children to play, and someone else had brought a chess-set and was already concentrating.

Mrs Ferguson seemed quite at home, and gave a little talk about 'Liverpool in the old days'. She could remember the 'Great War' with Germany.

"Of course there was no bombing then," she said." Except when they sent their silly air-ship over London – what was it called... Zeppelump or something – and we all know what happened to that!"

Tim's Mum explained. "It was called Zeppelin and dropped a few bombs before it was 'punctured' by our Royal Flying Corps and brought down."

Cakes and drinks were passed around and there was a quiet buzz of conversation. It was almost like a party, and Tim soon forgot that he had been in disgrace only the night before, entering into the spirit, and helping himself to several cup-cakes. It felt like one big family. Everyone was anxious, but tried not to show it, and did their best to cheer each other up. They sang some of the soldiers' songs…"It's a long way to Tipperary', and 'Pack up your troubles in your old kit bag and smile, smile, smile'. But it wasn't easy to smile as they sat and waited.

Almost thirty minutes passed by and there was no sign of any raiders.

"Perhaps they aren't coming, after all?" Shirley whispered.

Then they heard it…the same angry drone of bomber engines passing high overhead on their way to the docks, followed by the sound of distant explosions. It seemed worse than the night before.

"I think Herr Hitler's trying to finish us off," someone said.

"But he jolly well won't!" declared Mrs Ferguson defiantly, holding Charles close. "…will he, Charles?"

Charles yawned.

Almost everyone was holding somebody else now.

Mum held Shirley close.

Tim said he was 'alright', which wasn't true. He had read his last Beano and had been doing some thinking. 'What would happen if one of the stray bombs fell on our shelter? Is the concrete roof thick enough?' Suddenly it dawned on him that they might all be in great danger. 'And another thing…was Mr Impitt right? Were the bomb-aimers targeting the railway line…and what if they scored a direct hit? If so, the 'Scot' mightn't run past the end of Welbeck Avenue for months or even years, which would be a tragedy for hundreds of train-spotters!'

There was no singing now. People just sat close and whispered.

Then in the quietness there was a shrill, eerie whistling noise followed by a gigantic thud which shook the shelter floor and made the dim lights flicker and the bunk wobble.

"That was very close!" said Mr Impitt. "It's a good job it was a dud…that's when the mechanism doesn't work, so the bomb can't explode," which everyone had already guessed. "But it can still do an awful lot of damage," he added, gloomily.

Now everyone was thinking 'Did it land on a house and, if so, was it ours?' No one dared go outside to look.

"Well, that's that!… it's back to Colemere tomorrow for you two," said Mum, which wasn't good news, either for Shirley, who was determined to stay with Mum and Dad, bombs or no bombs, or Tim, who was desperate to stay around to hunt for more shrapnel, to make up for his lost nose-cone.

The sound of the bombers died away, and not long afterwards the 'All-clear' sounded. The shelter emptied quickly, as everyone made their way home, hopefully, through the darkness.

When the Olivers reached the house, Mum opened the back door very carefully and felt her way slowly along the hallway to check that the house was all there still. She gave a big sigh of relief. The 'dud' had missed number 6.

Shirley and Tim followed on tip-toe, and were on their way to bed when there was a loud knock on the front door. It was the warden who had met Tim the night before.

"Sorry, missus," he said to Mrs Oliver, "but you can't stay here. There's an unexploded bomb three doors up, at number 12. Please get your sleeping gear together and leave the house straightaway. Dovedale Road School is open, and you and your family can spend the night there. We'll tell your husband where you've gone, and let you know when it's safe to come back."

Mrs Oliver wasted no time in packing an over-night bag, and they set out for the school, with a quick look-back at number 12. The whole of the front had disappeared, as if an enormous hammer had smashed it from top to bottom. On the upstairs floor Mrs Ferguson's bed and wardrobe were, miraculously, still in place, and in the downstairs front-room her chaise-longue and a framed picture of Dixie Dean had also survived; but Henry's cage and several other items had gone from sight.

There was a gaping hole in the front garden and the pavement, and nestling in the mud was Adolf Hitler's ugly present to Welbeck Avenue. The warden had already put a cordon around the hole and the police had cordoned-off the end of the Avenue, to stop curious sight-seers coming too close.

"Poor Mrs Ferguson!" said Mrs Oliver.

"And poor Henry!" said Tim. "I hope he's alright."

Mrs Ferguson was standing at the end of the Avenue clutching Charles. She was quite sure that Henry had become a 'casualty of war' and, in between sobs, was saying some pretty strong things about 'Mr Hitler'. She was waiting for her sister, who lived in West Derby on the outskirts of the city, to come and take her to stay the night with her. But she was determined to be back the next morning 'to see that horrid thing taken away!'

The Olivers set out for the school, Tim carrying his football and a few Beanos. Billy and his Mum were already there, with some of the other Welbeck Avenue folk. There were mattresses on the floor of the gym and the two families settled down for the night next to each other.

After breakfast in the school dining-hall the boys wandered around, enjoying having the school to themselves, with no one to boss them about. They swung on the ropes and climbed the wall-bars in the gym for a few minutes and, in their classroom, Billy stood by the teacher's desk and did his popular impersonation of Mr Donaldson.

"Tim Oliver, your homework is sloppy! Write out 'I must not do sloppy homework', fifty times."

But they were keen to see the action back at Welbeck Avenue and said they would go to the park for football, which was true; they didn't say that they would go past the end of the Avenue, which was also true, but wouldn't have been allowed.

A small crowd had gathered by the cordon, looking anxiously towards number 12. Mrs Ferguson had already arrived with her sister, a large lady called Beatrice. She was pointing up the Avenue towards her ruined home, announcing, in her most defiant voice, that it would take 'more than a Nazi bomb' to frighten her.

The boys edged up to the policeman at the cordon.

"Can we have a look at the bomb, please?" asked Billy. The bobby frowned.

"There's a five hundred pounder lying down there, my lad," he replied, "and if that goes off, it could take a couple of houses with it - and two nosey lads as well, if you don't keep well away."

"Spoil sport!" Billy whispered, and they ran off towards the park.

Not long afterwards, two soldiers from the Bomb Disposal Unit climbed down among the bricks and glass and pieces of furniture, including the remains of Mrs Ferguson's cocktail cabinet, which she had inherited from her great aunt, and to which she was very attached. Henry was down there too, making a dreadful fuss, which was hardly surprising, considering that he had spent the night there in his cage, all alone in the dark.

One of the soldiers picked the cage up, scrambled back up to the street and placed it carefully on the pavement as Henry continued to complain. Mrs Ferguson was overjoyed and almost fainted.

Now came the scary part. The soldiers wore head-guards and carried heavy metal shields for protection; but everyone knew that, if they made a mistake while they were trying to make the bomb safe, there wouldn't be much hope for them.

While they waited, the crowd stood quietly, whispering to one another, as if they thought that a loud word might disturb the bomb. The minister from the little chapel around the corner said a prayer for the soldiers and there was a quiet chorus of 'Amen' from the crowd. A goods train rumbled slowly past the end of the Avenue, unaware that there was danger nearby.

It took nearly an hour for the soldiers to defuse the bomb, but at last they climbed out onto the street and gave the signal that it could be taken away. Now it was safe for the crowd to cheer, and everyone wanted to shake hands with the brave men, who waved and drove off to the next dangerous job.

Mrs Ferguson dashed up to reclaim 'POOR DEAR HENRY!' She was crying and laughing at the same time. She still had her beloved parrot and half of her home, even if she couldn't live in it for a few weeks; and now she had an exciting episode of her own to add to her store of 'true Liverpool tales'. Henry seemed to have recovered from the shock of being hurled into the crater without any warning, in the dead of night; but the cabinet would never be used for making cocktails again.

Now all the Welbeck folks could go back to their homes, except for Mrs Ferguson, of course, who was surrounded by neighbours inviting her to stay with them while her house was being repaired. She could take her pick, but decided to go and stay with Beatrice, as it would be too upsetting to think of her ruined cocktail cabinet every time she went to the shops.

By this time Shirley and Tim were on their way back to Crab Mill Farm with Mum, as Bill Brett's car wove its way towards the city centre, zig-zagging through piles of rubble and skirting around cordons guarding great, gaping holes.

Now they could see the mess the bombers had made when they missed the docks. There was glass and rubble everywhere, charred timbers still smouldering, and shops with no windows, where workmen were putting up boards. One notice announced

'NO WINDOWS, BUT BUSINESS AS USUAL'.

Here and there they spotted a gap in a row of houses, like a missing tooth, where a bomb had had a direct hit, and high up in a block of flats the outside walls had been completely blown off, leaving bedrooms, lounges and kitchens open for everyone to admire the wall-paper.

Shirley pointed.

"Look! It's just like my doll's house with the front taken off!"

Curtains waved about in the breeze, pictures hung lopsided, and furniture lay precariously at an angle, as if it might slide off and crash to the street at any moment.

In one room there was a table with its cloth still in place, and the door had been closed.

"Look!" Shirley pointed again…"there's a teapot and a cup and saucer. Someone was probably having a nice cup of tea when the siren went. It's a good job they didn't stay to enjoy it!"

Tim grinned.

"I bet they were surprised when they went back and opened the door!"

"It's so strange looking into other people's houses," Shirley said quietly, "… I mean without being invited."

They drove on past a wide open space where there should have been a whole row of houses, but now there were just mountains of rubble – bricks, beams, windows, and broken furniture…cupboards, lamps and pictures; and people rooting around sadly, looking for treasured belongings.

"That was a land-mine," Bill Brett muttered quietly. "They're monster bombs intended for the docks; but if they land in the wrong place they can blow away a whole row of houses as if they were made of matchsticks!"

"It must be awful to lose your home and belongings like that," Shirley said. "I wonder where all the people will go to live?"

"Their families will probably take them in, or neighbours," Mum replied. "It's a strange thing about danger and disaster – it often makes people kinder…and can bring them closer to each other, like everyone chatting and singing and cheering each other up in the shelter last night…and I'm sure Mrs Ferguson didn't realise how many friends she had, until this morning!"

They drove past the majestic sandstone Cathedral which the bombs had missed altogether, on through wide open spaces in the city-centre where, only a day or two before, there had been impressive shops and offices which they hadn't missed, and past St George's Hall, with its 'guardian' lions like those in Trafalgar Square. Tim pointed.

"They're not afraid of German dragons!"

Soon they were on their way through the tunnel and out past the ship-building yards where they were racing against time to build motor-torpedo boats and other fighting-ships. There was rubble everywhere until they reached the open country, so the journey to Colemere was slow.

At last they pulled up outside Crab Mill and sat down to tea, as they had done when they first came, almost exactly one year before. But Bill Brett was already glancing at his watch, and soon it was time for the Morris to take Mum back before the black-out.

Now the evacuees knew how dangerous it would be for Mum and Dad back at Welbeck Avenue, so the 'goodbyes' took much longer.

As she was getting into the car, Mum handed a parcel to Tim.

"Here's something to cheer you up, Tim."

Then, once again, the car was heading back up the lane, and Tim ran up to the top yard, climbed onto the hay cart and opened his parcel.

Inside he found his Meccano box, and inside, wrapped in tissue paper, was the precious nose-cone and a little note.

> Dear Tim,
> Enjoy showing your ugly bit of
> bomb to your country friends –
> and behave yourself!
>   Love, Mum

He yelled 'Yippee!' and ran to find Joe.

****

Geoff didn't come back to Crab Mill Farm. Mrs Everson said that she couldn't look after three evacuees properly, but she had found him a good home at the Stokes' farm in Lyneal.

They were all very sorry, but knew they would see him at school.

CHAPTER TEN

RUN RABBIT, RUN!

To Joe's surprise, Tim was quite cheerful as they walked up The Drive to the school. It was the first day of the new term. Now he would be in class 2 with the older kids, and kindly Miss Beddoes would be his teacher. So he had escaped from the Dragon, he thought.

Unluckily for Tim, however, the Headmistress and Miss Beddoes had exchanged classes, as they did every year, so there was no escape after all.

At break-time they were in the playground.

"It inna' fair!" Tim growled.

Joe agreed. "But at least we'll be in class two together…and it's harvest, so there'll be some fun after school. Dad's cuttin' the wheat in the big field today, and the other lads'll be there."

"What'll they be doing?"

"Rabbit runnin'!"

"What's that?"

"Well, the rabbits like to visit the wheat for a free lunch, but if they're helpin' themselves when the cuttin' starts, they're trapped. Some of the clever ones make a run for safety straight away, when it's not far to the hedge. But a lot stay around until there's only a bit of the wheat left to hide in and it's a long way to the hedge…that's when the runnin' starts…and the fun, unless you're a rabbit!"

"What happens?"

"Well, you walk alongside the tractor and cutter, but not too close, and watch the driver - it'll probably be my Dad. When he spots a rabbit near the edge of the wheat, he'll point to 'im. Then you've got to look lively, 'cos he'll come out and make a dash for the hedge, and it's our job to catch 'im before he gets there...and you munna' forget to shout. That frightens 'em and sometimes they look for a stook to hide under."

"What's a stook?"

"It's standing a few sheaves together - they're bundles of wheat tied up with twine - a bit like a Red Indian teepee. It lets the wind blow through to dry the wheat. That's Bob and Gerry's job."

"So what d'you shout?"

"Oh... 'Yah yah yah'... that sort of thing... anythin', as long as it's loud!."

"What do you do then... I mean, if you catch one?"

"You hold 'im tight by 'is hind legs and give 'im a sharp whack behind 'is 'ead with your stick."

Tim pulled a face. Billy Thompson kept two pet rabbits, named Monty and Maisy, in his back yard, and Tim was allowed to give them a carrot or lettuce leaf to nibble.

"That's a bit cruel, isn't it?"

"We dunna' think so. My Mum says it's wartime now, and there wunna' be enough food to go around, so we've got to eat the rabbits...and anyway, they've been havin' a good time gettin' fat on our wheat... and rabbits are good at dodgin', so they've got a good chance of gettin' away."

Tim still wasn't sure he liked the idea of frightening the rabbits and whacking them; but chasing them sounded too much fun to miss, so he was waiting at the gate after school, when Joe shot straight past him.

"Come on, slow coach" he shouted over his shoulder, "it'll all be cut before we get there!"

Tim caught up and they ran on down The Drive together. As they got nearer to the field they could hear the clicking sound of the cutter. They perched themselves on the gate to get their breath back, and a few moments later some of the other village lads climbed up and joined them.

It was Crab Mill's biggest field – about four acres, Joe said, rectangular in shape and surrounded by hedges and bushes. The 'cutter' was working its way around the wheat, taking a slice off each time. Joe's Dad was driving. He saw them and waved.

By now the island of wheat had already shrunk in size, and Tim was wondering how many rabbits were huddled together, waiting for the right moment to make a dash for safety.

He had heard a song on the wireless...

Run, rabbit, run, rabbit, run, run, run;
Don't give the farmer his fun, fun, fun.
He'll get by without his rabbit pie,
So run, rabbit, run, rabbit, run, run, run!'

He grinned. 'So that's what Joe meant!'

The late afternoon sunshine was hot. They took their pullovers off, rolled their shirt-sleeves up and stockings down, then took up their positions not far from the cutter.

Mr Everson was doing his best to drive straight and keep on the look-out for rabbits at the same time.

Suddenly he pointed, as one little chap came out of the wheat and scuttled right past Gerry. He dropped the sheaf he was holding and made a dive for it; but it was too quick, and disappeared into the hedge.

Tim gave a little cheer to himself, and was so busy congratulating the rabbit on its clever escape, he didn't notice another which had made a speedy exit from the wheat, close to where he and Joe were walking. They both saw it at the same time and gave chase, 'yah-yahing'. Then it did a sudden 'U' turn, and, as they tried to do the same, Joe tripped over a sheaf and Tim tripped over Joe.

They lay there on the stubble, watching, as their quarry reached a bramble bush, and the last they saw of it was a white tail disappearing into a friendly burrow. It was the rabbit's turn to have some fun, and reminded Tim of Brer Rabbit's clever escape into the 'briar bush' from the clutches of Brer Fox.

Gerry had been watching and laughed.

"Dunna' keep too close to the tractor, lads!" he shouted, "then you'll have a better chance of cuttin' 'em off before they reach the hedge."

They took his advice and jogged along on their toes, about half-way to the hedge, keeping their eyes on Joe's Dad. Tim's heart was beating fast and the rabbit song was going round and round in his head. Suddenly rabbit pie sounded delicious, and he had forgotten all about Monty and Maisy.

'Joe's right. This is fun!'

Now there was only a small rectangle of wheat still standing, about twenty paces long and ten paces across, and Mr Everson began pointing.

"Watch out!" he shouted... "here they come!" and at that moment three or four rabbits darted out of the wheat and ran for their lives, followed by others. Tim imagined that they had held a last-minute discussion and decided that it wasn't safe to stick around any longer.

There was pandemonium. Joe's Dad pointing and shouting "over here!" and "over there!", lads scampering up and down, yelling at the top of their voices, and rabbits heading for the hedges in every 'do or die' direction. Tim's head was buzzing. His problem was deciding which one to chase, but by the time he had picked one, either it had almost reached the hedge, or was being chased by someone else. He was beginning to think that he wasn't cut out for rabbit-running.

Then he spotted one which had poked its head out of the wheat on the side furthest away from the hedges. It had very long ears with black tips, and looked particularly plump, as if it had spent too long at its free lunch.

'This could be my last chance,' he thought. 'He's got a very full tummy and the longest distance to run, so perhaps he'll get tired before me.'

Then the contest began. The quarry looked left and right as if it was doing its road-safety drill, sniffed the air, and set off towards the distant hedge. Tim took a deep breath and went in pursuit. He noticed that it seemed to have extra-long back legs and was surprisingly good at dodging the stooks and hurdling over sheaves. But Tim was getting quite good at dodging and hurdling too.

As he ran, he heard Mr Everson's voice… "Go, Tim, GO!"

But this one was faster than he looked; its long legs seemed to be eating up the distance to the hedge too quickly, and Tim had almost given up the chase when he gave one last, desperate yell and, to his great surprise, it disappeared into the middle of a stook.

Tim ran up and followed it, head-first. He could just see one long hind leg and made a grab for it. It kicked like mad, but he held on and lay there for a few moments wondering what to do next. Then he decided that he needed help.

"Joe!" he yelled from the middle of the stook, and his friend ran across.

"I've caught one, but I canna' hold him."

Joe grinned.

"No wonder," he said. "He's a hare!"

"Well, whatever he is, Joe, I canna' hold him much longer!"

"Give 'im here," said Joe. He held the hare by its hind legs, lifted his stick, and as Tim closed his eyes, gave it a hard whack behind its head. It stopped wriggling and lay still on the stubble.

"That's how you do it!" said Joe.

Tim opened his eyes and stood up. His knees were scratched and sore from the stubble, but he didn't mind that. He looked down at his catch.

"Poor chap," he muttered. Then he picked it up by its long hind-legs, and they set off across the field to where the other lads were sitting. All the wheat was cut and the fun was almost over.

Joe's Dad was standing by the tractor as the boys walked by, Tim proudly holding his catch up so that the farmer could see it.

"Well done, Tim!" he said. "I reckon that fellow thought he would easily beat you to the hedge, but you surprised him. If it had been on a flat field he would have won, but the stubble and stooks slowed him down. He was probably sorry he'd eaten too much of my wheat!"

The other lads were resting in the shade of a big tree, sharing a drink from a bottle. Tim's throat was dry and sore from yelling, and when it was his turn he took a big gulp, bubbles flew up his nostrils and he spluttered.

"What is it?"

"Cider!" they all laughed.

"We have it every harvest," said Joe. "It's a special treat and part of the fun!"

"It's strong stuff, made from best Crab Mill apples." said Mr Everson. "Not for schoolboys really. But I think you've earned it!"

One of the other lads looked across. "That was good running, city boy!"

The city boy grinned.

The 'catch' was laid out in a row on the stubble. There were eight rabbits and Tim's hare. They were divided up so that each family had one and Bob and Gerry had one each. Tim was allowed to take his hare back to Crab Mill.

It was getting dark as they headed for the farm and went into the kitchen with Tim's catch.

Mrs Everson smiled.

"So you've caught your first rabbit, Tim, and I see it's a hare! You're turning into a real country lad. We'll keep it in the cold room for a pie when your Mum comes for your birthday."

At supper Tim could hardly keep his eyes open. Then he went straight to bed and fell fast asleep, dreaming of rabbits with very long legs leaping over giant stooks.

CHAPTER ELEVEN

SHOOTIN'

"There must be an easier way of catching 'em," said Tim, through a cloud of sherbet.

It was the next Saturday morning. They were sitting on the gate into the top field, watching Shep trying to sneak up on a group of rabbits without being noticed, and without success.

"If only my Dad would let us use his shot-gun," said Joe." You canna' miss when twenty bits of lead-shot fly out of the barrel!"

"We could make a catie," said Tim

"What's that?"

"You know - a catapult! They're dead easy to make. My friend Ken's got one. My Dad dunna' agree with them. He says they're dangerous, specially for kids; but if I tell him it's for shooting rabbits for the war effort, I don't think he'll mind. We'll need special elastic. I'll ask my Mum to bring some when she comes on Friday."

That afternoon he wrote a letter home, with a request for the special elastic. Then they went into the wood to find the thin branch of a hazel tree, with another branch coming off it, in the shape of a capital letter Y. They cut the branch off three inches below the fork to make a handle, and three inches above the fork to make two 'arms'. Now they just needed a pouch to hold the 'bullet', and the special elastic. They pestered Joe's Mum for some old canvas, and cut a rectangular piece out, to make the pouch, and when Tim's Mum arrived, they were at the bus stop to meet her.

"This is an honour," she smiled. "A double escort!"

"Well, we thought you might need some extra help with your bag, Mum," Tim grinned.

"And I suppose you're wondering if I've got the special elastic!"

She laughed, to keep them in suspense.

"Well, you're in luck," she said, pulling a bulky package from her handbag.

Tim tore the wrapping paper off to reveal a length of thick, black elastic.

"It's like liquorice!" Joe laughed.

"An' just what we need!" said Tim.

Back at the Farm they cut the elastic into two pieces, each ten inches long, then tied two ends to the arms of the Y with string, and the other ends to the pouch.

Now they had got their catapult.

"We need some target practice," said Tim.

"And I know just the thing," said Joe. He led the way to the upper yard to rescue a churn from the nettles, and stood it up against the milking shed wall. Then they hunted around under the hedges for stones of the right size to fit the pouch.

Tim thought that he should have the first shot, as it was his elastic. He slipped a stone into the pouch and stood sideways on, feet apart for balance, about five paces from the target. Holding the catie at arm's length and making sure that the churn was 'sitting' in the arms of the Y, he pulled the pouch back and fired. The 'bullet' fell short.

"A bit more muscle, city boy!" cried Joe.

Tim frowned. He fitted another stone, took aim, pulled the pouch back as far as he could, and fired. The stone flew straight to the target and there was a loud 'clang!'

"Good shootin'!" shouted Joe, and Tim grinned modestly.

Then it was Joe's turn, and he was soon making the churn sing. Now they were ready to bag a few rabbits for the war effort.

"Mornin's the best time," said Joe. "There's always lots in the top field."

The next morning, after breakfast, the two hunters crept across the lower yard and up towards the hedge surrounding the top field, with a pocketful of assorted stones and the catie safely tucked into the top of Tim's shorts. He was excited, and thinking how dull it would be back at home with only sparrows and the odd pigeon to shoot at.

The field was quite crowded at that time of day, as Joe expected, and the happy rabbits were either nibbling the grass or playing a rabbit version of leap-frog, with no idea of the danger that lurked on the other side of the hedge.

Joe licked his forefinger and held it up to the wind.

"Let's go downwind," he whispered and pointed, "...so they won't sniff us and run off."

They stooped low and crept along behind the hedge until they reached a spot downwind from the rabbits. Tim fitted a stone into the pouch, peeped over the hedge, took aim at the nearest one, and fired. The stone flew high and wide, and the target went on nibbling. He tried again, but by this time it had moved further away, and the shot fell short.

"Drat!" he frowned.

Then it was Joe's turn. There was another group sitting on a grassy hump not far away, too busy nibbling to notice the hunters. He took careful aim at a particularly fat one and fired. The stone just missed, but that was the signal for them all to head for safety, and by the time he had reloaded, they had relocated to the far side of the field.

He muttered a word which he had heard Bob and Gerry use when they were annoyed, and which he wouldn't have wanted his Mum to hear; and Tim, who had been learning some new words in the farmyard himself, agreed. Hunting rabbits, even with a high-powered catapult, wasn't as easy as it seemed.

"Now they know we're here!" Joe sounded annoyed again.

They decided to try the next field.

"I'll do a recce," said Joe, "... to check if there are any around." He stooped low again and made his way along the hedge; then he stopped and beckoned to Tim.

Tim crept along to join him.

"There's a whole lot sittin' just by that gap," Joe whispered, and pointed. " We canna' miss! If we can get close enough we should get a couple of good shots."

They had almost reached the gap when Joe put his finger to his lips and pointed at the group of sitting targets. Now it was Tim's turn again. He was humming the 'rabbit pie' tune to himself, and as he loaded the pouch, he was determined to make the next shot count. He stood up slowly to pick a target; but at that moment one of the senior ones sniffed the air, looked across, and spotted him. It thumped its rear paws, which was the signal to head for home, and just as Tim let fly, they took off across the field. The stone whistled after them, but if it did hit one, it was only on its backside, and made it move even faster.

It was the same every time they picked a new target. Either it was too far away, or wouldn't sit still.

"It's no good," Joe moaned. "We're never going to bag one."

Tim agreed. It did seem hopeless. But he had gone to a lot of trouble to get his catie, and was determined to prove to Joe that, with some practice and a bit of luck, a well-made catapult could be almost as accurate as his Dad's shot-gun. So every day, after school, the catie stayed in the top of his shorts for when they found an interesting target, if possible one that didn't move.

Their chance came a few days later. They were in the churchyard shovelling a pile of coke for the church boiler, and the catie was in its place on Tim's hip. They had finished shovelling and were heading through the graveyard towards the lychgate, when he noticed the stones on the path...smooth, clean, medium-sized, perfect for catapults!

Then he spotted the vases on the gravestones...some posh ones with fresh flowers, and quite a few ordinary jam jars, empty and dusty.

He picked one up.

"Look at this, Joe. What a great target!" He scooped up a handful of stones. "And look at all this ammunition! Let's have pot-shots!"

Joe looked startled.

"We canna' do that in the churchyard, Tim! My Dad's the verger, remember!"

"But it's only a jam jar, and nobody bothers about them. We can stand it on top of that headstone." He pointed to a very old, overgrown grave. "It's just the right height."

"But it's somebody's grave, Tim...and our shootin' inna' very accurate. Suppose we damage the words?"

"That's easy," Tim grinned. "We'll shoot from the other side. Then we canna' damage 'em."

But some words were going round in Joe's head... words they said every morning at assembly...'Lead us not into temptation.'

"...and suppose it smashes."

That was exactly what Tim had in mind.

"It'll be more fun!"

"Well...promise we'll pick all the bits up."

"Promise!"

"Just one or two shots then!"

Tim stood a jar on top of the head-stone. Then he loaded the pouch, took careful aim, and, as Joe looked away, he fired. The stone flew straight to the target and the jar exploded.

"Bull's eye, Tim!" said Joe, glancingly nervously towards the lychgate. "But we'd better pick the bits up and go now."

But Tim wasn't going.

"This is fun, Joe!" He stood another jar on the headstone. "Your turn!"

But Joe wasn't having fun, and his hand was shaking badly as he took aim and fired. The stone flew high over the target and into the field beyond.

"Bad luck, Joe! Have another shot," cried Tim, and he was stooping to pick up a stone, when a voice came from the direction of the lychgate.

"Is that Tim Oliver?"

The boys froze, as the speaker walked up the path towards them. It was their friend the Postmistress.

"I thought it was you, Tim," she smiled. "I could recognise a Liverpool lad's voice anywhere..."

She stopped as she spotted the jar on the gravestone and the broken glass all over the ground. Her bright smile disappeared.

"Whatever have you two been up to?"

The boys stood looking at the ground, but the catie was still in Joe's hand, and it didn't take the Postmistress long to answer her own question.

She looked at Joe.

"Joe Everson," she said. "I canna' believe that you would come and play games in the churchyard, and you the verger's son!" Then she looked at Tim.

"And you, Tim Oliver! I know you're away from your Mum and Dad, but this is a bad thing to do. I'm very disappointed."

The boys continued to look at the ground.

"Well, you must do two things," she continued. "First you must pick up every piece of glass that you can find, and then..."

They froze again. They could guess what the second 'thing' would be.

"You must go and tell Joe's Dad what you've done."

Joe gulped.

The Postmistress went to get a brush and shovel from the church vestry and left them hunting for the broken glass. Then they trudged slowly back to the farm to find Joe's Dad.

He was in the dairy, fixing the milk-cooling system.

"We were in the churchyard shovellin' the coke, Dad," Joe began, "...and we had pot-shots at a jam jar with Tim's catie...and smashed it..."

"And...we're very sorry," added Tim.

The farmer said nothing and went on with the repairs, while they stood waiting and worrying. After a few minutes he turned and looked at them.

"That was a disgraceful thing to do, and you should know better, Joe. The churchyard should be a place of peace and beauty, not a fairground. Now go and spend some time thinking about what you've done, while I think about a suitable punishment."

A few minutes later they were in the upper yard, thinking.

"It was all my fault, Joe," said Tim. "I didn't mean to get you into trouble with your Dad."

Joe shrugged. "But I could've said 'No'."

Before supper they went back to the dairy to hear Mr Everson pass sentence.

"That overgrown grave where the jar was broken," he began, "is where some of Mrs Brown's relatives are buried, and she's in a wheel-chair, as you know, Joe, so she canna' look after it. On Saturday morning you must take a spade and hedge clippers, and tidy it up for her. That'll make the punishment fit the crime, as they say in court. No need to tell anyone why you're doin' it – that'll be between you and me. But you'd better go and tell the vicar what you've been up to. "

They nodded.

"And Tim, when your Mum and Dad come to visit, you must

own up to them."

It was Tim's turn to gulp.

After supper they ran across to the vicarage. The vicar came to the door.

"Hello, boys," he said. "I suppose you want to see James?"

"No," said Joe. "We've got something to tell you, vicar."

"Well, you'd better come in then." Mr Pye led the way to the study.

Tim had never seen so many books. They were everywhere, and where there weren't books there were photographs of cricket teams featuring the vicar in his younger days. On the mantel-piece next to the clock there was a solitary cricket ball mounted on a plaque with an inscription

Presented to Arnold Pye to mark his ten wickets taken for the Old Grampians against the Old Paladians June 15th 1908

In a frame over the fireplace was a verse from the Bible…

'Run the race ahead with endurance, keeping your eyes on Jesus'

Tim guessed that the vicar had chosen it because cricket isn't mentioned in the Bible.

The two offenders perched themselves on the edge of the well-worn sofa and waited for him to open the innings.

"Now, what can I do for you? Not another battle with the Lyneal lads coming up, I hope!"

Joe did the talking again, while Tim sat and fidgeted and the vicar listened. When Joe had finished, the three sat in silence.

The movement of the clock on the mantel-piece sounded very loud. Every now and then the vicar said "Mmm…" or something like it, and drummed with his fingers on the arm of his chair. At last he spoke.

"That was a strange thing to do in a churchyard, boys, and I can see that you are very sorry. I'm also grateful to you for helping to ensure that the church will be warm for Sunday services this winter.

So…" He frowned at them across his desk in a judge-like way, then smiled. "…your punishment will be to come and bowl at me next summer, when I'm practising my batting for the church fète!"

"Phew!" said Joe, as they walked down the drive. "I thought he would at least give us a little sermon!"

The next Saturday morning anyone passing the churchyard might have noticed two boys tidying up Mrs Brown's family grave, and thought 'What kind boys – and one of them's an evacuee!'

That afternoon Tim's Mum and Dad came to visit and he had decided to get his confession over as soon as possible. So he was waiting at the bus stop as they got off the bus, and, bearing in mind that his Dad didn't agree with catapults, he hoped it might help if he started by explaining that the main reason for making one was to shoot a few rabbits to help with the war effort. He also mentioned that the reason that he and Joe had been in the churchyard in the first place was that they had been doing a job for the vicar. But it didn't help.

Mum had a little cry, which made him feel worse, and the kind of storm that he feared most, gradually gathered on his Dad's face.

"You are a guest in Colemere, Tim," he said, "and you've let everyone down. I've told you before…catapults are dangerous things and can get people into all kinds of trouble. You tell me that you've already been punished, but I will keep the catapult."

He held out his hand.

Tim took the catie from its 'holster' and handed it to him.

The shooting season was over.

****

Nor was Tim having much success at school. The other evacuees who had gone home at Christmas had come back to reclaim their desks, so he was in his old place at the back of the class; and even more evacuees were arriving. Shiela Cullen and her three very lively brothers James, Keith and Brian had come to stay at Mistletoe Cottage in Colemere with Mrs Smith. They were from Liverpool, too. That was three more good reasons for not paying attention.

CHAPTER TWELVE

ELI'S STORY

"We have another new pupil with us, today," the Headmistress announced importantly in assembly one morning.

"His name is Eli Fieldsend. He has come from Birmingham, although his home-country is Germany. So he's an evacuee like some of you. He has come a long way, and I want you to be friends with him."

They all looked at the new boy and thought he looked a bit sad. At play-time Joe and Tim went up to him.

"Hello, Eli" said Joe, "I'm Joe, and this is Tim. He's an evacuee, too."

"Hello, Joe," Eli smiled. "Hello, Tim."

"Why did you come to our country, when Germany's our enemy?" Joe asked, quite politely.

"I came before the war," Eli replied. He spoke slowly and pronounced each word carefully. "My parents said I would be safer in your country."

"But that doesn't make sense!" said Joe. "If Germany's your country, why weren't you safe there?"

"Because my family is Jewish, and our nation's leader, Adolf Hitler, says that Jews are not proper Germans, and are not wanted."

"What did he mean?" asked Tim.

"My father says it is because we are different."

"In what way?" asked Hilary Sykes.

Already a little crowd had gathered around to listen.

"Well, we have not got a land of our own, like everyone else. We did have a great empire once... but that was long ago and, ever since, our people have lived in someone else's land."

"Well, there are lots of Jewish kids in my school at home," said Ted Lister. He was a new evacuee from Stoke-on-Trent. "The only way they're different is that they have lots of holy days and get off school, so they're very lucky! They're clever, too, and good at lessons!"

Eli went on. "My father says that many Jews have important jobs, which makes Hitler jealous. He says it is our fault that Germany has been poor for many years. My father says that is not true, because Jews work very hard, for themselves and Germany. But many people believe what Hitler says."

"Some of his followers - they are called 'Brownshirts' - started to bully us. My grandfather is a clock-maker. He has a shop near the centre of the city, and in school holidays I did little jobs for him. One day, while I was wrapping up a clock, some of the Brown shirts came in and started shouting at him. He is quite old and was frightened. I was frightened, too. They snatched the clock from me and threw it on the floor. Then they painted the star of David – that is our sign – on the windows, and 'Down with the Jews!' I saw the same words on other shops."

"Is that the star of David?" Isabelle Edwards was pointing to a small badge on Eli's jacket. It was like two triangles, one on top of another making a six-pointed star.

He nodded.

"Wasn't he the boy who killed Goliath?" Ruth Hinton asked.

"Yes...and he became our greatest King."

He continued...

"Another time the Brownshirts marched into the synagogue - that is our Church - and beat the Rabbi - he is our priest. They took the holy scriptures out and made a bonfire with them. Then they set fire to the synagogue. The flames could be seen all over the city. The fire burnt all night and in the morning there was nothing left."

"Why didn't someone send for the fire brigade?" asked Don Williams.

"They did, but it did not come."

"Why not?"

"My father said they were probably afraid of the Brownshirts. They do what they like and nobody tries to stop them. One night they went around smashing the windows of Jewish shops all over the country. It was called Krystalnacht...it means 'night of crystal'. It was very frightening."

He stopped talking and stood quietly for a few moments, then went on.

"The government made a law that Jewish children are not allowed to play with the other children, and one day my best friend, Jurgen, said he could not be friends with me any more. I asked him why, and he said 'Because you are a Jew, and my parents say I am not supposed to be friends with Jews.' I think he was really sorry, but he had to do what his parents said...in Germany, children are always obedient to their parents."

"Doesn't anyone stick up for the Jews?" asked Betty Egerton.

"Yes, some people do. One of my school friends told me that the minister of his church spoke against the new laws and the bullying, and the police went to his house. They told him to stop, or he would be in trouble. My father told me that some ministers have been arrested and sent to special prison camps.

"The secret police – they're called Gestapo – started to arrest our people, even though they had done nothing wrong. It was usually at night-time. They were put on special trains and nobody knows where they were taken. My mother told me that some of our friends have made secret hiding places in their homes, behind cupboards and walls and places like that. She said that if I heard a loud knocking on the door in the night I must hide in the attic at the top of the house. But it would not have been any good. They know where to look."

"My parents were really afraid, and said they must send me away to somewhere safe. I did not want to leave, but I knew they would only send me away if they had to. My aunt Ruth – she is mother's sister – lives in Birmingham and said she would look after me if I could reach her."

"How did you come to England, Eli?" asked Robert Williams.

"Some kind people arranged for special trains to take Jewish children out of Germany, and my father found a place on one of them for me. At the station my mother was crying as if she thought she would never see me again. My father told me to get on the train and not to look back."

He stopped speaking again for a few moments.

"The train stopped at the border. The Brownshirts were everywhere. They looked angry. I think they did not like us getting away. We were frightened, and our carers told us to 'just sit quietly'. We were very hungry and thirsty. Some ladies gave us food and drinks through the windows. We were very tired too, because we could not sleep properly. We were on the train for three whole days. Then we got on a ship at Amsterdam which brought us to England. My Aunt was waiting for me, and brought me to Birmingham. I was lucky. One boy told me he did not know who he would be staying with, or if anyone would have him."

"Aunt Ruth took me to a school near her home and told the Headmistress about me. I had some good friends, and I learned to

speak English quite quickly."

"Then we heard that Britain was at war with Germany and Aunt Ruth said that Birmingham has many factories working for the war effort, so it would not be safe for me to stay there. She has kind friends at The Yetchleys in Lyneal, who said I could stay with them. That is how I came here."

He stopped.

"Will your Mum and Dad come and visit you, Eli?" asked Shirley.

"I hope so," he replied. "Aunt Ruth has written letters asking them to come and live here if they can get away, but they do not reply. She is very worried. I am too."

The crowd listening to Eli's story was big by now and everyone stood quietly.

"Where will you go to church, Eli?" Muriel asked. "I don't think there's a sinagong – or whatever it's called – near here."

"There is one in Birmingham," he said, "but it is too far away."

"You can come to our church in Colemere, if you like," said Joe. "The Reverend Pye is the vicar. He's keen on cricket...but I don't suppose they play cricket in Germany."

He pointed to James.

"This is his son, James."

"I'm sure my Dad would be pleased if you wanted to come, Eli," said James. "I heard him say that Jesus, our Saviour, was a Jew. He would say some prayers for your Mum and Dad…and your Granddad."

Eli smiled in a sad kind of way.

"Do you play football?" asked Tim.

"Yes," he nodded. "All German boys play football. But I like running best."

At that moment the bell for lessons rang, and everyone filed back into school.

****

At lunch-time Eli was with Joe, Tim, Ted and some of the others in the playground.

"Let's play fox and hounds," said Ted.

"What is fox and hounds?" asked the new boy.

"It's a chasing game. One of us is the fox and goes and hides. The others give him a start, then try to find him and catch him before he gets back to school – that's his den."

"May I run with you?"

"As long as you can keep up," said Tim.

Eli grinned. "I will be alright!"

"Who'll be the fox?" Ted asked.

"I will," George Hanson volunteered.

"Right," said Ted. "Get going, George! We'll count to a hundred, and then we'll be after you."

George ran off down the road towards the canal, which was about four hundred yards away. Soon he reached a bend in the road and was out of sight, but could still hear the counting, '58, 59, 60, 61…'

At the canal he crossed the hump-backed bridge, then stood still and listened. The counting had stopped. The hounds would be hot on his trail.

Now he needed a good hiding place, and, not far from the bridge there was a large coppice of trees. He picked out an oak, perfect for climbing, and pulled himself up onto a branch just as the 'pack' came pouring over the bridge.

He sat very still, not daring to move.

"Look on the paths," someone shouted, "…he might have left a trail."

They were all running in different directions now.

Then Ted shouted "Look in the trees," and the fox knew that, if they spotted him now, he was trapped. He dropped to the ground and darted back over the bridge and up the lane towards the school and 'sanctuary'.

There was a loud yell. "There he goes…after him!" and the next moment the hounds were in pursuit.

Now George had volunteered to be the fox because he was a good runner, and he had his plimsolls on; but as he glanced back over his shoulder he got a shock. The new boy was ahead of the others, and starting to catch up on him.

George was out of breath, but fifty yards from the school gate he put on a final, desperate spurt, and had almost reached the gate when a hand grabbed his shirt.

"Gotya!'" said a Birmingham voice with a German accent.

The fox was caught, and the new hound was grinning all over his face. The rest of the pack was only a few yards behind.

"Good running, Eli!" said Ted. "Did you learn to run like that when the Brownshirts were chasing you?"

Eli's grin disappeared, and Ted knew that that wasn't a good joke.

"I was one of the best runners in my school, and I practised a lot," Eli said. "My father showed me pictures of the American athlete, Jesse Owens. He won four gold medals at the Olympic Games in Berlin, and one day I would like to run like him."

CHAPTER THIRTEEN

EGGS AND ANGELS

It was Saturday morning and there was time to doodle. Tim had asked specially if they could have the four largest eggs in his week's haul for breakfast. He scraped the last bit out of his egg and gulped it down. Then he turned the empty shell upside down in its cup and, as the others watched, began to draw a face – eyes open wide and staring, nose, ears, extra large mouth, as if it was always shouting, a little moustache, like Charlie Chaplin's, and black hair sloping downwards towards the left eye.

When he had finished, he put his pencil down and stood up, held out his right arm, fingers together, pointing straight ahead and slightly upwards, put his left index finger under his nose as a moustache and announced, in a loud, pompous voice..."Heil Hitler!"

The others turned their empty shells upside down and started to draw. When they had all finished, they knew exactly what to do.

They picked up their spoons, stood up, did the Nazi salute, shouting "Heil Hitler!' and bashed the egg-shells. Large cracks appeared, bits of shell flew everywhere, and everyone cheered, except Mrs Everson who was looking at the mess.

They were busy clearing it up when Mr Everson came into the kitchen. He smiled when he saw the egg shells.

"I see you've been givin' Adolf a headache!"

"Yes, Dad," said Joe. "As an EGGSample!"

They all laughed, but the farmer was looking serious now.

"Well, he's throwin' everythin' at US at the moment. He seems to think he'll make us give in by bashin' us with bombs!"

"Will we, Dad...give in, I mean?" asked Muriel.

He frowned. "No, we wunna! Mr Churchill says that if the Nazis ever come here, we'll fight them wherever they go...on our beaches...in our streets, and in our fields. We wunna' ever give in!"

He spoke quite loudly, and they all looked at him in surprise. But Mrs Everson was nodding. She understood that the proud farmer hated the thought of Nazi soldiers marching all over England, especially his precious little bit of the Shropshire countryside. He continued.

"But the battle's in the sky now, and everything depends on our fighter-pilots. Mr Churchill says that if they lose this battle, our Christian civilisation might end."

Everyone sat quietly and the egg-shells stayed a few more minutes on the table cloth, which looked quite like a battlefield itself.

"I wish we could do something, don't you, Joe?" Tim said.

"You keep huntin' eggs and flattenin' cans, Tim. That'll be your bit," the farmer smiled.

"But there's something we can all do," said Mrs Everson. "Tomorrow's Sunday. Let's go to church and pray for our brave pilots."

The next morning they all set out across the mere-field to the little parish church of St John the Evangelist.

Mr Everson had gone ahead to ring the bell. Before the war there had been four, but three had been taken down and carted off to factories with the tin cans, to be turned into bombs and bullets and things. The elderly Mrs Stokes did remind the vicar that the prophet Micah in the Bible mentions changing 'swords into ploughs', not church bells into bombs, and the vicar had listened sympathetically; but it made no difference. Three had gone, and the one that was left was supposed to be rung 'only in the event of an enemy invasion'.

However, the church council had agreed that, 'on this Sunday, the bell shall be rung for one minute, to remind everyone to come and pray'.

Police Constable Lewis, the local bobby, wasn't at all sure.

"We dunna' want everyone thinking that Nazi paratroopers might be dropping onto the mere-field at any moment," he said; "but as this is a time of national danger, I suppose it'll be alright."

So the sound of the one bell rang out across the mere, over the ridge to the village, across the wheat-field, and up The Drive to Lyneal for exactly one minute and, when the Crab Mill family reached the churchyard gate, it looked as if everyone wanted to be in church. There was a queue at the door and almost every seat was already taken.

"There's always a few spaces at the front," Joe's Mum whispered, and he led the way and found an empty pew, just big enough for five, right next to where the vicar would be standing. Tim had never sat so near the front in church, but as he and Joe had only recently sat on the vicar's sofa and were good friends of the vicar's son, he guessed that it was probably alright.

The vicar entered wearing his most cheerful outfit and smiled down at the children in the front row. Then he gripped the pulpit firmly and spoke solemnly.

"As we all know, these are dangerous times for our nation. A powerful, evil enemy is not far away. At this very moment our young pilots will be in the skies" – he waved an arm towards the church rafters – "defending our land against their bombers, and this is a good place to be at such times, helping with our prayers."

They sang a hymn...'*He who would valiant be 'gainst all*

disaster'. Tim remembered it from school and thought it was a good one to sing.

Then the vicar began his sermon, and Tim began to day-dream. There was a pretty girl on the front row of the choir. He wondered what her name was, and thought that perhaps he should come to church more often. Then he started to count the number of angels in the stained-glass windows. He wondered if angels have caties and play football, and, if so, do they have leagues in heaven?

Then the vicar said something that woke him up.

"'Love your enemies and pray for those who treat you badly'."

Tim frowned and looked across at Joe, as if to say 'Did you hear that?' Then in his mind, he began to argue with the vicar.

'Do you mean we should love Adolf Hitler...and the Nasties who spend all their time treating people badly... are we supposed to pray for THEM? And what about Charlie and his gang? What good would it do to be nice to them?'

But the vicar seemed to know what Tim was thinking, and continued...

"Loving your enemy isn't the same as liking him. It means trying to understand him, and doing your best to be friends. If it's not your fault that he's against you, it means trying your best to forgive him."

Now Tim was thinking about the broken egg-shells.

The vicar went on. "Of course, doing our best to be friends with everyone doesn't always work, and that's when people and nations fall out and sometimes go to war."

Tim remembered the tired gentleman on the wireless. He had tried so hard to persuade Hitler to leave Poland alone, but he took no notice.

The sermon ended and there were prayers - for the King and Queen and princesses, Mr Churchill, the brave, young pilots and the cities being bombed, 'including Liverpool' Tim whispered under his breath. Then the vicar glanced down at the front row and prayed a special prayer 'for the evacuees, that they'll be happy with their country Mums and Dads,' and Mrs Everson said a loud 'Amen!'

After the service the others walked back up to the farm and Joe and Tim stayed by the mere-side, skimming stones. There were lots at the water's edge - round and flat and smooth, perfect for skimming, and Joe held the record of twenty-four bounces. Then they took their shoes and socks off and sat at the end of the jetty cooling their toes.

"I think it inna' easy to be a Christian," Tim said.

"No, I think it inna'," said Joe.

They sat leaning back against the railings, thinking and swatting midges.

"I wonder what would happen if the Nasties ever come to Colemere?" said Tim.

Joe thought for a moment.

"Well, there's the Home Guard at Ellesmere. My Dad's joined up. He's got a proper soldier's uniform and a gun. They have shootin' practice behind the Black Lion on Wednesday. "

"That sounds fun," said Tim. "Pity we're too young."

"We could hide," said Joe. "I know a great place in the wood. It's a sort of cave. I've never been inside 'cos it's very dark, and I think there might be bats; but nobody would ever find it. I'll take you."

After lunch they trotted down the main path through the wood and came to a spot where the trees were thickest. Joe hesitated for a moment, trying to remember the way, then plunged into the bushes and started climbing towards the ridge. At times they were on all fours, grabbing branches and tree roots to stop their feet slipping. They had almost reached the ridge, and suddenly found themselves in a small clearing. A group of spindly pine trees was dotted about, and a thick carpet of needles covered the ground. On the far side of the clearing there was a wall of rock jutting out from the ridge, and high up on the face of the rock they could just make out a hole not much bigger than the entrance to a badger's den, half-hidden by a bush.

"That's it...that's the cave!" Joe pointed, and they raced each other up the rock-face to reach it. Tim got there first and knelt down to peer inside. Then he drew back.

"You're right, Joe. It's really dark!"

Joe had remembered to bring his torch and swept the inside of the cave with the beam. There was no sign that people or animals had been inside, and if there had been bats they had moved somewhere else.

He squeezed through the entrance and stood up. Tim followed. Their eyes soon became used to the darkness and they could make a better inspection of their rocky hideout. The roof of the cave was well above their heads and the space was more or less square.

"It's perfect, Joe," Tim said, "and even if we don't have to hide here, it'll still make a great den."

By now it was almost tea-time. They pulled some of the branches of the bush across the entrance, slid down the rock face and headed back to Crab Mill.

After tea Tim scribbled a letter.

From Crab Mill Farm.

Dear Mum and Dad,

On the wireless it said that Liverpool is still being bombed, and I hope you are safe. Did the bin-men take Mrs Ferguson's bomb away? We heard it's the battle of Britain and our fighter-pilots are shooting lots of bombers down. Joe and me have found a great hiding place in case the nasties come to Colemere. I forgot to bring my Spitfire. When you come please bring it and some Beanos, 'cos we can't buy them at the Post Office.

Love Tim

A letter from Liverpool.

Dear Tim

Thank you for your letter. We are safe and well, although the bombing hasn't stopped. Mrs Ferguson's bomb has been taken away. Mr Impitt says it should be fixed and sent back with worst wishes from the people of Welbeck Avenue. The workmen are building a new front for number 12, and Henry has learnt a new word, which sounds like HELP!

Say hello to everybody at Crab Mill, and give Shirley a big hug from me.

Love, Dad.

CHAPTER FOURTEEN

FOE OR FRIEND

"I need a volunteer," said Mr Everson one evening after milking. "Gerry's too busy, and someone's got to deliver Mrs Fowkes' milk. It'll mean getting up a bit earlier, but there'll be an extra three pence pocket money each week."

Joe looked as if he hadn't heard what his Dad had said, and Tim wondered why he didn't seem interested in the offer of such a generous increase in his pocket money.

His Dad seemed to read Joe's thoughts because, after a few moments, he looked at Tim.

"How about you, Tim? It'll be a bit of extra war-effort, too. I'm sure your Dad would be pleased."

Tim hesitated. He was puzzled by Joe's silence, but couldn't say 'no' to the offer of so much extra pocket money.

"Yes, I'll do it."

"Good lad! I'll have a word with Mrs Fowkes. You can start tomorrow."

"Why didn't you volunteer, Joe?"

They were getting ready for bed, and Tim was looking across the yard towards the dairy where he would be reporting for his first milk delivery the next morning.

Joe was grinning.

"You dunna' know Mrs Fowkes!"

"What d'you mean?"

"She dunna' like kids. Her cottage is close to the canal where we swim sometimes, and when we jump off the bridge and make a lot of noise, like we always do, specially on Sundays, she comes out and shouts at us. She's a bit weird too. Gerry says she smokes a pipe, like the gypsies, and makes strange brews. When we go past her cottage we run as fast as we can…and sometimes we shout names. If I was you, I'd leave the milk at the end of the path and run!"

At seven o'clock the next morning there was a quiet knock at the bedroom door.

"Time for your milk-run, Tim," whispered Mrs Everson.

He rubbed the sleep out of his eyes, rolled out of bed, forgot about washing, got dressed and hurried downstairs.

It was only just daylight as he walked across to the dairy to collect Mrs Fowkes' daily pint. It was in a metal container with a lid.

"Now carry it carefully, Tim" said Mrs Everson. "Dunna' shake it about too much. Mrs Fowkes is especially fond of the cream on the top and wunna' be very pleased if it's mixed up with the rest of the milk!"

Tim nodded and, as he picked up the can, he felt one of his sinking feelings.

The quickest way to Fowkes' cottage was along the main path through the wood, the only tricky bit being the steep slope down from the farm to reach it, especially carrying a can of milk with a perfect layer of cream on the top. But once over the stile he made the descent successfully, steadying himself with his free hand on the ground, and after a few minutes' brisk walk in the fresh air, he reached the end of the wood.

Across the road sat Fowkes' Cottage. He hesitated for a moment, surveying the long, thatched building. A cloud of mist-like smoke hung over the garden, and the eye-brow windows seemed to be frowning at him. It made him think of Hansel and Gretel and the witch's cottage, except that this one wasn't made of biscuits and cakes, and that reminded him that he was hungry.

Now he wondered if he had made a mistake in volunteering. Should he take Joe's advice, leave the milk by the gate and run? But

Mrs Everson had told him to wait while the old lady emptied the milk into her jug, and bring the empty can back. He had to stay.

He crossed the road, lifted the latch of the garden gate and walked slowly up the path. The line of sun-flowers leading to the front door seemed like giant eyes peering down at him, as if to enquire why such a small person, who should still be in bed, was doing a grown-up's job.

The door was decorated with metal studs, like the doors of castles he had seen in books, and the knocker was in the shape of an owl, with wings extended and clawed-feet, ready to grab any unwary prey. Tim wasn't sure which part to take hold of, but decided to try its beak, which he lifted and brought down as gently as possible. Perhaps whoever was inside wouldn't hear it, and he would have a good reason for leaving the milk on the doorstep and going away.

He waited, still unsure whether to make a run for it or stay; but in less time than it took to glance over his shoulder at the escape route, which was the garden path, there was the grating sound of a bolt being drawn back, the door opened and there stood the awesome Mrs Fowkes.

He wasn't sure what he had imagined she would look like, but whatever it was, it was nothing like this. For one thing she didn't stoop or lean on a stick like the angry old ladies he had seen in story books. In fact she was quite dignified; her nose was normal, and she seemed to have plenty of teeth, although, on closer inspection, they were dark-brown coloured. To complete the surprise picture, she was wearing a multi-coloured, woollen bonnet on her head, not a black, cone-shaped hat; and the cat which had emerged from behind her was also multi-coloured, not black, and was rubbing against Tim's leg in a surprisingly friendly sort of way.

He took a deep breath.

"I've brought your milk, Mrs Fowkes."

The old lady put her hands on her hips and looked down at him as he stood holding out the milk-can with a shaky hand, hoping that the cream was still in place and that he wouldn't have to go any further. She reached out, lifted the lid, peered inside and nodded.

'Phew!' thought Tim.

She took the can from him, put it on a table and her hands back on her hips. Then she stood back to look at him again.

"So you're the new milkman Mr Everson has told me about," she said in a soft, rather low voice, "...and an evacuee, he tells me. Well, you're a bit small, but I dare say you'll do. Come on in, young man."

The young man hesitated.

"Come on," she repeated, " I won't bite!" and he thought he saw the whisp of a smile cross her face. His hand stopped shaking and he stepped through the doorway.

Straightaway his nose picked up the strong smell of tobacco and old carpets, and while the old lady skimmed the cream off and poured the rest of the milk into a jug, he looked around. He noticed a row of foxes' heads mounted on the wall over the wide fire-place, and frowned. A clay pipe lay on the table, bunches of strong-smelling plants hung from the low beams, and on a long shelf to one side of the fireplace there were several tall bottles containing a variety of coloured liquids. He guessed that they must be the 'strange brews' that Gerry had told Joe about.

The old lady put the lid on the empty can and handed it back to the new milk-man. He touched his forehead, which his Dad had told him 'gentlemen should always do to ladies, especially older ones,' and was edging slowly towards the door. He had almost accomplished his first milk-run without being eaten.

"Just a minute, young man!" said Mrs Fowkes. She took the lid off a tin box, picked out a biscuit and handed it to him.

"I dunna' suppose you've had breakfast, so you must be hungry, gettin' up so early. It's ginger and blackberry - to give you strength to climb back up that ridge!"

"Thank you, Mrs Fowkes," said Tim, and quickly made his way down the path under the giant eyes, the empty can rattling in time with his steps, across the road into the wood and back to the farm, to prove to Joe that he had survived.

"She was quite nice, really."

"That's because you're new… and you didna' make a noise or call her names!"

So Tim began his second country career – as a milkman.

The next Saturday there was an extra biscuit to nibble and some

questions to answer in return, mostly about his home town. The old
lady could remember the boy scouts and the excited voices echoing
'all the way from the mere-field' through the wood as far as her
cottage.

She had never been to a big city, she said.

"And I wouldna' want to either, especially now there's a war
on! Ellesmere's big enough for me."

He asked about the foxes' heads, and she explained that her son
John, who worked on the Oteley Hall estate had 'smoked 'em out and
shot 'em!' Tim said he thought they had nice faces and 'dinky' little
teeth, and it seemed a pity to shoot them.

"They're pests," she said, "especially in the summer. They go
into the wheat after the rabbits and do a lot of damage…that's when
they anna' gettin' those dinky teeth into the chickens!"

It was his first 'pay day', and back at the farm he picked up
his wages after breakfast and made tracks to the Post Office. A six
penny 'tanner' could buy so much more than a joey. Country life was
getting better and better for him and Joe, who had also got an extra
job, delivering milk to old Sam. It was his Dad's way of treating the
boys fairly.

The next day was Sunday, there was more time to chat, and his
new friend had another question for him, as she put her jug down and
looked at him with a gentle, curious smile.

"I should think you miss your Mum and Dad a lot?"

"Yes… sometimes," he replied "…mostly at bed-time. That's
when Mum reads to me, and Dad, too, if he gets home in time; and
they say a prayer. But Mr and Mrs Everson are so busy with the
farm, they haven't got time for stories. And anyway, Joe and me are
always so sleepy, we just want to put the light out." He paused for a
moment.

"When we hear about the air-raids I worry a bit, and hope
they're alright. My sister worries all the time."

The old lady nodded.

"And I'm quite sure your Mum and Dad worry about you and your sister every single day, and pray for you."

"Yes, I s'pose so," he said quietly, almost to himself.

"Well, you'll be quite safe here in Colemere, my young friend, and happy too, I hope."

****

There were the jobs to do after school, too. Joe's Dad said he should be 'extra vigilant' with his egg-hunting 'now that they're rationed'; and Joe always needed help with Sheriff. So when he climbed into bed he was soon fast asleep, and didn't hear the drone of bombers high up above the peaceful countryside. Colemere seemed to be right under their flight-path and, on clear nights, Mr and Mrs Everson stood at the farm-house door, watching them as they headed north on their deadly missions and, later on, hurrying back to their bases in France.

CHAPTER FIFTEEN

A NEAR MISS

They were all at breakfast one morning when Mr Everson hurried into the kitchen.

"A bomb fell in Lyneal last night…they say it might have landed on the school. The postman told Mrs Hughes and she told Gerry as he was on his way to work."

"Why would the Germans drop a bomb on our school, Dad?" Muriel asked.

"They wouldna' do it on purpose," he replied. "But when a bomber's got one of our night-fighters on his tail, if he hasn't reached his target and has some bombs left over which would slow him down, he'll drop 'em anywhere, just to get away. Usually they make a big hole in a field somewhere, but sometimes they land on a building… like a school."

"It's a good job it was during the night," said Joe, "or we might have been in class."

"And killed!" Tim added, to frighten the girls.

As they finished their breakfast, everyone was trying to imagine the school in ruins, and Tim was thinking 'NO SCHOOL! That means NO LESSONS!' He was even thinking nice things about the German pilot for doing all the kids a good turn. And another thing…where there's been a bomb there should be shrapnel!

After a very quick breakfast he loaded the shrapnel box into his satchel. Joe hadn't finished feeding Sheriff, but Tim couldn't wait, so he set off for the school, or what was left of it.

He reached The Drive, and looked through the tunnel hoping to see an empty space where the school had been standing. But it was still there. The postman and Mrs Hughes and Gerry had got it wrong.

If a bomb had fallen on Lyneal village, it certainly didn't land on the school.

As he got nearer he slowed to a trudge. One or two windows had been broken by the blast from the explosion; otherwise it was all there, and the Headmistress was standing calmly by her desk, as if nothing had happened. He didn't want her to notice how disappointed he was, so he pretended to smile cheerfully and went straight to his place at the back.

Everyone was chattering about the bomb, and, at assembly, the Headmistress said how thankful they should all be that it had missed the school. 'Not me!', Tim thought. It had landed just down the road, she said, and she hoped that Mr Williams wasn't too upset by the big hole in his field.

Meanwhile Tim was already laying his plans.

At play-time the boys met up in the playground.

"I'm going shrapnel-hunting after lunch," Tim said. "Who's coming?"

"What's shrapnel?" asked Archie Lewis.

Tim frowned. Surely everyone knew about shrapnel, even country lads.

"It's the bits of a bomb that fly everywhere when it explodes!"

He told them about the night he had gone out hunting for war souvenirs 'with enemy bombers right overhead,' which wasn't exactly true, but sounded more exciting. Then he opened his box to show them the nose-cone.

"That's not very interesting," someone said. But Tim took no notice. He wouldn't understand that Tim had risked his life to find it.

Archie Lewis and Joe said they would go, and so did Ted who was always looking for a bit of adventure. Eli said he didn't want to look at the mess a Nazi bomber had made in the field. Don Williams said he would go along as it was his Dad's field; and some of the others said they would think about it.

Tim ate his lunch quickly and was waiting at the gate when Ted came across with Joe, Archie and Don and the five ran down the road to farmer Williams's field.

Constable Lewis had looked at the crater earlier that morning. He had never seen a bomb crater, and wasn't sure what to do about this one, but he thought it might help if he tied some coloured tape across the gateway to show that it had been officially checked. Then he went home for breakfast, and seemed to have forgotten about it.

The boys reached the gate and Archie looked at the tape fluttering in the breeze, then towards the crater.

"Are you sure it isn't dangerous?" he asked.

"Of course it isn't!" said Tim. "It's already exploded, hasn't it?"

They clambered over the gate and trooped across the field with Archie following at a safe distance. The explosion had thrown up a huge mound of soil all around the crater. They scrambled up the sides and stood quietly for a few moments, looking down into the hole.

"It's like a volcano!" Ted gasped.

"You could put a house in it," said Archie.

"What are we supposed to do, Tim?" asked Don.

"We climb down, then get on our knees," replied the shrapnel expert, "and feel in the soil with our fingers." He had never done it

himself, of course, but someone had to give instructions; and he didn't see how else anyone could hunt for shrapnel in a big hole in a field.

"Be careful, though," he added with a bit more authority,"'cos shrapnel's sharp."

The five slid down into the crater on their bottoms and started digging. The soil was soft and moist, and soon their hands and knees were dirty. Once or twice an excited voice said "Here's something!" but it was just a piece of slate or stone.

Half an hour went by, their fingers were getting very tired as well as dirty, and they still hadn't found anything. Even Tim began to feel like giving up.

"It's hopeless," said Joe.

"And we're going to be late for lessons," added Ted.

Tim gulped. He had forgotten all about lessons.

There was a quick scramble back out of the crater, over the gate and up the lane to the school. The playground was empty and the clock over the main door said five past two.

Afternoon lessons started at a quarter to.

As they entered the classroom, all the other pupils turned to look at them, and then at the Headmistress, who rose to her feet slowly and majestically. The five stood in a line, hiding their hands behind their backs. They couldn't hide their knees, and Archie's were trembling. Don was biting his lip, wondering what his Dad would say, Joe seemed to be examining the ceiling, and Tim was crossing his fingers. Only Ted, who loved a bit of excitement, was keeping calm.

"Where have you been?" Mrs Low asked, in her special 'I'm in charge here' voice.

There was a long silence. The voice continued.

"...You are twenty minutes late for lessons. What is your excuse?"

Everyone in the classroom held their breath. Some sniggered. Charlie and his chums smirked. Shirley raised her eyes as if to say 'He's in trouble again!'

At last, because it was his idea, Tim spoke up.

"Please, miss, we've been looking for shrapnel in the crater."

"What was that you said?" The Headmistress's hearing wasn't very good. Tim repeated himself a bit louder, which made it sound worse.

"WE'VE BEEN HUNTING FOR SHRAPNEL IN THE CRATER, MISS."

Now the Headmistress pulled herself up to her full height, so that she could really look down on the five criminals.

"Who told you that you could leave the school...and how dare you go into Mr Williams's field? Didn't you see the tape PC Lewis put across the gate...and just look at your knees." That was four crimes for a start, and there was more sniggering, specially from Hilary, who hated Tim because he wouldn't let her play football with him.

"Hold out your hands!"

Five pairs of grubby hands were held out as the Headmistress sailed across to her desk and picked up a wooden ruler. Then she walked along the line, and there were ten short, sharp sounds as the ruler came down on ten hands.

"Now let that be a lesson to you all," she said.

Then she looked down at Tim.

"I see that your leader is an evacuee. Well, you aren't in a big city now, Timothy Oliver, and I won't have you getting our country boys into trouble."

Tim looked at his feet as the voice droned on...

"I have far too many pupils in the school, now that you evacuees have arrived, and I cannot watch every one of you. HOWEVER, (she said the word slowly and loudly)...in future I will be watching YOU, Timothy...VERY carefully!"

"Yes, miss," Tim muttered, although he thought of saying "HEIL, miss!" He was almost crying. It wasn't because his hands were hurting. They were just a bit sore. But he hated being called Timothy, especially in front of the whole class.

At play-time everyone crowded round in the playground asking questions. "What's shrapnel?"..."Did you find any?" and Tim picked out Hilary's voice…"Did the ruler hurt, TIMOTHY?"

At play-time the next morning the boys were practising hand-stands against the school wall. Suddenly Geoff shouted.

"Look!" He was pointing at the wall. It was at the end of the school facing the crater-field and there, just above his head, was a big, round hole, deep in the brickwork, and below it, on the ground, were small pieces of brick and powdered cement. Everyone crowded around.

"I know what would make a hole like that," Tim yelled… "something very hard and sharp, moving very fast…something like SHRAPNEL!"

"But it didn't go through the wall," said Joe, examining the hole, "so it must still be here somewhere."

There was a scramble to search the playground, but no sign of the missing shrapnel.

"It must have rebounded off the wall," said Ted. "Look over by the hedge, everybody!"

Now there was a rush to search the hedge and, at last, an excited voice shouted "GOT IT!" It was Archie, grinning and holding up a large lump of metal, grey coloured, with jagged edges. Everyone crowded around again.

"It dunna' look much like a bomb," someone said.

"Of course it dunna'," said Tim, who was fed up with explaining. "It's just a piece of bomb. That's what they do – just explode into pieces and fly all over the place."

"So what should we do with it, now we've found it?" asked Ted.

"It belongs to us all, in a way," said Don.

"Why dunna' we start a museum – a sort of war museum?" said Archie. He sometimes had a bright idea, and everyone agreed that Archie, Ted, Joe, Tim and Don should go and tell the Headmistress about this one.

She was drinking her morning cup of tea when the committee

knocked on the kitchen door.

Archie held out his hand to show her the shrapnel.

"We found this in the playground, Mrs Low. It's a bit of the bomb. It made a hole in the school wall."

The Headmistress peered at the chunk of metal as if it was a kind of slug, and sniffed.

"If the wall hadn't been in the way," said Joe, "it might have hit Miss Beddoes' cottage, and she might have been injured … or even killed." He spoke solemnly. Miss Beddoes was a lot younger than Mrs Low, and much prettier.

The Headmistress looked quite startled.

"Dear me!"

"We thought we could start a museum, miss," said Tim, "…a sort of war museum."

Mrs Low glanced at him, and again at the chunk of metal.

"Well, I can't say it's very beautiful, but if there was a card explaining what it is and where it came from, it would make a very good centre-piece – and a reminder to us all that our little school had been in the war. But you will need some more exhibits. We can't have a museum with only one, can we?" She almost chuckled. "Have you any other ideas for your museum?"

"We can use my gas mask," said Ted. "My Dad says they probably won't be needed in the countryside."

"Well, we can't be too sure about that, Edward, can we?" Ted looked a bit crestfallen.

"What about a ration book, Mrs Low?" asked Don, "once the coupons were used, I mean."

"We could have a map of England showing where all of us evacuees came from," Ted chipped in, "and one of Lyneal and Colemere showing where we all stayed."

"Well, I think it's a very good idea" said Mrs Low. "So now you'll have to start collecting. If you need my help, come and tell me."

Then she looked at Tim.

"So your sad story will have a happy ending, after all, Timothy," she said, and sipped her tea.

"Yes, miss," muttered Tim, and trudged off to join the others.

****

A letter from Tim to Billy.

Dear Billy,

A bomb nearly fell on the school, but it missed which was a pity'cos we would we would have had a few weeks off. We found a chunk of shrapnal from the bomb. Mrs Lowe says we can start a musseum. Are you doing any train spotting? There aren't any for miles around Colemere. Just the station at Ellesmere. It is a single line so the engines have to push one way and pull the other. It's my birthday next week. It's a pity we can't have a party. Say Hi to the others.

Your friend Tim

A letter from Wrexham.

Hi Tim,

I'm sorry the bomb missed the school. Danny ran away. He got up early but didn't get very far along the Chester Road. He was hungry, so he ran back just in time for breakfast so nobody notised or he would have got into truble from Mr Danaldson. Some nights we can hear the bombing and I say a prayer for my Mum and Dad and yours. I read the Wizard now.

Sid and Ken say hi and happy birthday!

Your friend Billy

CHAPTER SIXTEEN

SPY IN BLACK

Tim perched himself on the old mile-stone a few yards from the bus stop. It should have said '**Shrewsbury 12 miles**', but PC Lewis had painted over it. Joe's Dad's Home Guard platoon had been busy, too, turning the signposts at all the road junctions to point the wrong way; so the one saying '**Ellesmere 3 miles**' now pointed to Loppington.

"That'll fool 'em," said Mr Everson, and the boys thought it would be fun watching Nazi soldiers strutting off down the road in the wrong direction.

Tim had run most of the way from school, to be in time to meet the 4.20pm bus from Ellesmere. Mum and Dad were coming to celebrate his ninth birthday, and he had asked Shirley if he could meet them by himself.

He fidgeted a bit on his makeshift seat, his eyes glued on the road from Ellesmere. He was feeling a bit annoyed because, if it hadn't been for the war, he would be having a party with Billy and the others back at Welbeck Avenue.

The bus arrived right on time, and even before she got off he recognized his Mum by the little orange-coloured hat she liked to wear when she visited, slightly tilting to one side, with a long, gingery feather. There was no sign of Dad.

Tim was waiting at the bottom step and they hugged.

Mum smiled sadly.

"Dad's so disappointed that he couldn't come for your special day, Tim, but the bombers are still targeting the docks most nights, and every single fire-watcher is needed." Tim frowned, but nodded to show he understood. Then he grabbed her suitcase, and she knew what he was thinking.

She smiled. "I've got a special birthday surprise for you, Tim, but it's not in the suitcase. You'll have to be patient and wait until the morning to find out what it is."

Shirley had been waiting by the pump and ran to meet them. After long hugs they strolled on down the lane chatting.

"Mr Everson says the Nasties have been throwing everything at us," said Tim.

"Yes, they have, Tim. They sent hundreds of bombers over, in great waves. The sky was black! At times there were four enemy planes to every one of ours! But our fighter-pilots were ready for them. They kept climbing back into their cockpits to go up to meet them and either shot them down or made them turn back. So Herr Hitler had to think again!"

****

Tim was up extra-early the next morning, and ran most of the way to Fowkes' cottage. He had worked out a way of carrying the milk at speed without disturbing the layer of cream, by holding the can out in front of him with his arm slightly bent at the elbow, so that it wouldn't be jolted.

The old lady noticed that he was out of breath.

"You're early this morning…and in a hurry, I see!"

"Yes, it's my birthday…I'm nine today."

"Nine! That's nearly double figures," she smiled, "and deserves something more than a biscuit, I think."

She went over to a cupboard and rooted around inside, humming a little tune to herself. Meanwhile Tim was admiring the foxes' teeth, and trying to read the names on the bottles of her special brews, such as Walnut and Crab-apple Cider, Damson and Dandelion Delight, Gin and Ginger Special (for adults only) and Pear and Peppermint Cordial.

Mrs Fowkes soon found what she had been looking for. It was wrapped in a piece of dark-green cloth. She placed it on the table,

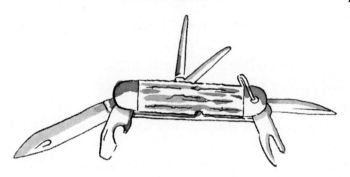

pointed to it, and stood back with her hands on her hips, as usual.

"Open it, young man," she said.

Tim obeyed, and lying there was a pen-knife, although he had never seen one like it. The handle resembled the bark of a tree; it had different blades for cutting, and a variety of gadgets, including one like a small knitting needle.

"That one's for taking stones out of horses' hooves, and things like that," she explained. "Now that you're getting to be a country lad, you should have a country lad's pen-knife! It belonged to Mr Fowkes, my dear husband. He left it here when he went to France to fight in the last war; but he didn't come back, and it's been in that cupboard ever since. I think he would have liked you to have it."

Tim grinned. "It's amazing! Thank you, Mrs Fowkes. I promise I'll take care of it...and I'm very sorry about Mr Fowkes."

"Oh, it was a long time ago, and there were so many who didn't come back" she said sadly.

"But this is your birthday, and not a time for sadness!" she smiled. "So you'd better run, or you'll be late for the celebrations!"

He wrapped the knife in the cloth, picked up the empty milk-can, and ran down the garden path to the road. The old lady stood by her door listening to the rattle of the can, filling her pipe and humming her tune.

When he ran into the kitchen, everyone was waiting for him and he was proudly showing off the various blades and gadgets of the amazing pen-knife, when he noticed that Joe was looking a bit glum.

"We can both use it, Joe. I'm sure Mrs Fowkes would be pleased."

Joe wasn't sure, but cheered up anyway.

His 'country' family gave Tim a model of one of the 'Merchant Navy' class of express trains.

Tim gasped. "It's amazing!" which was his new favourite word for something special.

Shirley had made a pencil case from material she had in her work basket, with the letters TO embroidered on it.

"I thought you'd need it for school, Tim," which was true, because he was always losing his pencils.

He grinned. 'Just like a sister!'

Generous Auntie May, who loved sweets herself and wanted everyone to love them, had sent a large, mixed bagful. Grandma Oliver had sent a pair of mittens in bright purple wool. Tim pulled a face.

Mum frowned.

"You should be grateful, Tim! Grandma unravelled one of her favourite cardigans especially, to knit them for you. She says we can't buy them in the shops now and, in winter, Shropshire is often the coldest place in England, so you'll need them."

"They're just what I wanted," said Tim, grinning at Joe.

There was a book – *Every Boy's Book of Aircraft Recognition*.

"Dad chose it specially, to go with your Spitfire" said Mum. "It's to help pilots to recognize another aircraft by its shape, in case they can't see the emblem on its side or wings. That's why they're silhouettes, just outlines. So, in a 'dog-fight', when there are planes dodging about everywhere, our pilots won't shoot each other down!"

He flicked through the first few pages.

"It's amazing! We can test each other, Joe!"

"And now the surprise present", said his Mum, mysteriously. "This afternoon, I'm taking you all to the 'pictures' to see 'The Spy in Black'!"

Tim yelled "YIPPEE!" and jumped up and down. Going to the cinema was always a treat, even back at home where there were cinemas everywhere; but he guessed that to see a 'movie' in the middle of the countryside, especially a spy film, must be the best birthday present an evacuee could possibly have.

Mrs Everson already knew about the surprise, and had prepared an early lunch of hare pie, which gave the boys a chance to tell the story of how they had chased and 'bagged' it themselves.

They caught the 2.10 bus so that they would be at the 'cinema' in good time. It was really the Town Hall, an impressive building in the town centre, which they called 'The Plaza' when films were being shown. The notice outside said...

SHOWING TODAY!

The Spy in Black

Starring
CONRAD VEIDT

and Tim was jumping up and down again, until he spotted the queue. It stretched right down the High Street, into Wharf Street and out of sight. He gulped. After all the excitement, would they get seats? He crossed his fingers, but needn't have worried, as the queue moved quickly, and they soon reached the ticket kiosk.

Mrs Oliver bought the tickets and they went in to the noise. It sounded as if every kid in town, including lots of evacuees, had squeezed inside and was as excited as Tim.

They sat down just as the lights were dimmed and the projectionist went into action. The noise subsided, but only for a few moments before the words '**Battle of Britain**' came on the screen. The kids watched, open-mouthed, as German Messerschmidts and British Spitfires and Hurricanes chased each other all over the sky, climbing and diving, looping and rolling, the British trying to shoot

German bombers down, and the Germans trying to stop them.

The sky was criss-crossed with vapour trails, like a giant aerial maze.

Joe and Tim were trying to keep the score – but there was too much happening, and the noise made by the kids was as deafening as the soundtrack. Every time they spotted a trail of black smoke coming from an enemy plane as it nose-dived into the ground, they stood up and cheered and stamped. Now Tim was really enjoying himself, and Joe looked at him in surprise, as if to ask 'Do city kids always behave like this?'

Tim just grinned and went on stamping.

At last the caption came up –

ENEMY LOSSES 163

Someone had kept the score after all, and Britain was safe for the time being, although the roof of the Town Hall was in danger of being blown off by the voices of two hundred happy children.

Then it was time for the 'Big Picture' and everyone sat down.

The Spy in Black was a German navy captain in a long, black coat who smuggled his U-boat into a Scottish loch with orders to blow up British warships anchored nearby.

The noise got louder again. When a German sailor came on the screen the kids yelled 'BOOOOO', and when a British sailor appeared they cheered.

The plot failed, and the spy was trying to escape, when his U-boat was accidentally attacked by another German ship and sunk, much to the glee of the young audience. The captain refused to be rescued and went down with his boat, and as they walked out, blinking, into the bright sunshine, Mum noticed that Tim seemed very quiet.

"I thought you'd be happy, Tim!"

"I was thinking…it's a pity the captain went down with his boat," he replied. "That was a brave thing to do."

"But he was a spy," she said, "and if he'd been captured he would have been shot; so he must have thought that going down with his boat was a more honourable way to die. And remember, Tim, if his plot had succeeded, lots of British sailors would have gone down with their ships, except that they would have had no choice. So don't feel too sorry for him!"

They walked on towards the bus stop, across the town square and past the Chemist's shop. A notice in the window said

'CARELESS TALK COSTS LIVES!'

"What does that mean, Mrs Oliver?" Joe asked.

"Well, the government is warning us to be careful what we say that strangers might overhear. There are enemy agents, spies, listening to try to pick up bits of information about our war plans, and they won't all be dressed in black, so they won't be easy to recognise."

"The only things people talk about in the country are cows and tractors and turnips and things," said Tim. "That wouldn't help the enemy much, would it, Mum?"

She smiled. "No Tim…but it would be very different in a seaport like Liverpool. Do you remember Mrs Simpson's son Harry,

over the road in Welbeck Avenue. He's in the navy now and will be
going to sea at any time. Well, suppose he was chatting with some
friends in the pub and happened to mention that his ship was sailing
on a certain day to escort a convoy across the Atlantic…and just
suppose the friendly-looking man nearby was really a German agent,
and heard what Harry said. He would send a message to Germany,
Hitler would send his U-boats to attack the convoy, and we would
probably lose a lot of ships and men, including Harry. That's how
careless talk costs lives."

"Will you warn Harry, Mrs Oliver?" Joe asked.

She smiled. "I'm sure he knows all about 'careless talk', Joe."

Just then the bus pulled up, and took them back to Colemere for
a tea-party with sandwiches and jelly creams. There was a cake with
nine candles and Tim was a very happy birthday-boy, although once
or twice he thought about the brave 'Spy in Black', and wished that
he had been on Britain's side.

CHAPTER SEVENTEEN

RATS AND RATIONS

The following Saturday morning after breakfast, Mrs Everson put four little booklets on the table.

"Bad news, everyone! The government says that sweets must be rationed, so you must each have one of these."

She handed out the booklets.

Tim frowned. Billy's Mum was right this time. Even sweets were rationed now. It was almost as serious as the bombing.

He glanced at his ration book. His name was printed on the front, and inside were what looked like sheets of postage stamps, although not so interesting.

"Now don't lose it, Tim," said Mrs Everson. "Even Mrs Hughes can't let you have sweets if you haven't got your coupons!"

At the Post Office the queue moved slower than ever. Now that they couldn't buy whatever they wanted, everyone was taking longer to choose.

A notice over the counter said

SWEET RATIONING
Each person is allowed Four Ounces
Per Week

"Is that all we can have, Mrs Hughes?" Tim asked, when it was his turn.

"I'm afraid so, Tim," she said sadly. "So you'd better choose carefully!"

She waited patiently while he made his choice, which wasn't

easy. It didn't seem fair. There seemed to be plenty of sweets, and he could have so few. He chose an ounce of Everton mints, a bar of toffee, a spearmint stick, a liquorice whirl and eight aniseed balls.

"No 'Five Boys' this time?" The Postmistress looked surprised. "Well, I think that's very wise, Tim. Sweets last much longer than chocolate!"

He watched closely as she scooped the mints from a jar into the bowl on one side of the weighing scales, slowing down to add them one by one, until the little brass weight on the other side of the scales gradually lifted, and the balancing arrow finally hovered just under the 1 OUNCE mark. She dropped one more mint into the bowl and the arrow moved fractionally over the mark. Tim crossed his fingers. Would she stick to the rules and put that last mint back in the jar?

Mrs Hughes glanced at the anxious customer, then picked up the bowl and emptied it into a paper bag.

"That one's for good measure!" She smiled.

"Thank you very much, Mrs Hughes," he grinned.

"That'll be four pence haypenny, Tim."

His grin turned to a slight frown. What good was an extra joey for his bit of war effort, if he couldn't spend it all?

He handed over five pence. The Postmistress took a coupon marked 30th September from his ration book and gave him a halfpenny change. He would have to save it to spend on more expensive rations the next Saturday.

While Joe was being served, he read the other notices pinned on the wall. On one there was a picture of a large, fat rat caught in a net. It said...

HAVE YOU SEEN THIS THIEF?

CATCH HIM AND TAKE HIS TAIL TO YOUR LOCAL POLICE STATION AND CLAIM THE REWARD

2d per tail

****

Back at the farm Tim went up to the upper yard to collect eggs. The chickens were laying well, and the morning's haul was eighteen. It was his best ever and he climbed onto the old tractor seat with his sweet ration, to celebrate.

Meanwhile Joe had gone across to the stable with Sheriff's morning feed of oats and, as he walked in, his quick eyes spotted a sudden movement in the big horse's feeding trough. He looked more closely, and there, in the middle of the trough, was a very large, round rat with tell-tale flecks of oat-meal on his whiskers.

Realising that he had been caught in the act of helping himself to Sheriff's precious rations, the intruder pulled himself up to and over the rim of the trough, somersaulted to the floor, dashed across to a hole in the wall and disappeared. Joe jumped backwards and tumbled to the floor. Sheriff shuffled about, but otherwise didn't seem at all upset. Perhaps he was used to sharing his daily bread with this unusual visitor.

Joe sat there thinking. How could a rat, especially an over-weight one, climb up a smooth wall to reach Sheriff's trough, four feet off the ground?

He emptied the oats into the trough and then went looking for his Dad, to tell him about the extraordinary, wall-climbing rat who was stealing Sheriff's grub from under his nose.

"How could he do it, Dad?"

"Oh, if they're hungry enough, they'll find a way to fill their stomachs," said the farmer. "They're very clever; but I dunna' think they're as clever as that! What I need is a Pied Piper – or two – to find out how he does it...and catch 'im."

"Tim and me'll have a try, Dad. "

Joe ran up to the top yard to find Tim and tell him about the clever robber-rat.

"We've got to find out how he gets in the trough, and set a trap for 'im."

"We can earn tuppence if we catch him," said Tim. "It says so in the Post Office. We just have to take his tail to Constable Lewis to prove that we caught him."

The next morning at Sheriff's usual feeding time, the boys tip-toed across the yard to the stable, hoping to witness the miracle of the wall-climbing rat. Tim stayed outside in the yard while Joe went in with the bucket of oats, which he emptied into the trough. Then he went over to the window which was covered with dust and cobwebs and made a small, round peep-hole in the dust, so that someone outside would able to see into the stable without being seen by whoever or whatever was inside, such as a hungry rat. Then he went outside, closing the door, and joined Tim, who already had his eye up to the peep-hole, as Sheriff made a start on his breakfast. So far there was no sign of the uninvited guest.

Then something startled the big horse and put the watchers on the alert. Tim put his finger to his lips and pointed towards a beam which ran high up across the stable from wall to wall, ending right over the trough. Joe took over at the peep hole just in time to see his friend from the previous morning scurrying along the beam. It reached the wall above the trough and paused, as if trying to pluck up courage, then leapt off the beam into thin air, and dropped straight into the trough, landing in a cloud of oatmeal. Sheriff took a couple of steps back from the trough and began to look on in an interested sort of way, while the intruder began to help himself to breakfast.

The mystery was solved. This chap didn't need to climb the smooth walls, like a lizard, to reach his free meal, even if that was possible. He had found a simpler, if more perilous way of gate-crashing the big horse's dining room.

The boys took turns at the peep-hole, as the rat helped himself from the trough, until he had decided that he had had enough for one morning. Then he pulled himself up over the rim of the trough, dropped to the floor, and exited speedily through the same hole in the wall that he had used when Joe disturbed him the morning before. Sheriff went back to his breakfast.

"Now we know how he comes and goes," said Joe, "and our job is to make sure that his next visit is his last."

"But how?" asked Tim. "We canna' set a trap on the beam. It's too high."

"We'll have to catch him on his way home," said Joe. "That hole must lead into the barn. Let's go and investigate."

They hurried around to the barn which was next door to the stable. Joe led the way up a ladder to an upper floor. Immediately he pointed to a hole in the wall.

"That's how our cheeky friend reaches the beam! But we know he dunna' come back that way."

They climbed back down the ladder, and Joe began to scoop up armfuls of hay from the floor.

"See!" This time he pointed to a hole at the bottom of the wall. "That's where he comes out. Now all we've got to do is to work out how to catch 'im."

All through supper, Tim was strangely quiet. He was thinking about rats. Joe's Dad said they're clever, and they knew that this one was extra clever.

Straight after supper he went upstairs with a pencil and pad, perched himself on his bed and began to draw. When Joe came to bed, Tim had a sketch to show him. It was of a wooden box with five sides, about a foot and a half long, a foot and a half wide and a foot deep, and a little door on one side.

"How does it work?"

"Well, we need a stick about fifteen inches long. We tie a piece of string to one end and some tasty food to the other end of the string. Then we use the stick to prop the box up, so the tempting food hangs down where he canna' miss it. When he tugs at the food, he'll pull the stick down, the box'll fall and trap him inside!"

"What's the door for?"

"It's so that we can open it and grab him."

"It looks good, Tim. A clever trap for a clever rat!... and Gerry's good at wood-work, so perhaps he'll make it for us."

They found Gerry in the milking shed, and showed him the diagram of Tim's invention.

"D'you think it'll work, Gerry?" asked Joe.

"I dunna' know, Joe. Rats are cunning creatures... and dunna' forget they can bite, too, especially when they're cornered. So if your trap works and you catch 'im, keep your fingers well away from his teeth!"

Gerry said he would 'knock the box together' and two days later it appeared, made exactly to the designer's measurements. A stick and a piece of string were much easier to find. All that was needed now was some tasty bait, and Gerry said a chunk of oat-cake would do the trick.

"The rascals love it!"

The next morning, straight after breakfast, Tim took the trap into the barn with a tempting chunk of oak-cake tied to the end of the string. He placed it a few inches from the hole which was the rat's escape route, and set it up according to his design, with one end of the box raised off the ground to allow a hungry thief to reach the special treat.

Meanwhile, Joe was serving Sheriff's breakfast. He emptied it into the trough, then retreated and took up his post at the peep-hole.

Right on time, as if someone had called out 'BREAKFAST!' their 'friend' ran along the beam, performed its aerial stunt, landing in the middle of the breakfast and, as Sheriff stepped back, started to munch.

Joe ran around to the barn where Tim was waiting. They climbed the ladder and lay down on the upper floor to wait and watch from the stair-well. In ten minutes they would have to head for school. The Headmistress was very strict about lateness.

The seconds ticked by and there was no sign of the thief. Then, at last, they heard a scuffling sound, and a nose with long, white whiskers emerged from the hole, followed by a plump body. The boys held their breath. Would he take the bait? Surely such rich pickings would be too tempting for any sensible rat to ignore. But, to the boys' dismay this one ran straight past the bait over to the door, and disappeared in the direction of the pond.

"DRAT!" muttered Tim. "D' you think he knew it was a trap?"

"Did he smell a rat, d'you mean?" Joe laughed. "I dunna' think so, Tim. He's probably eaten too much already, and it'll be the same every time he comes back with his tummy full! I think we've got the trap in the wrong place. Let's move it up here to the hole he uses on his way to Sheriff's dining room, so he'll be hungry when he spots it."

They carried the trap up the ladder and placed it near to the hole leading to the beam.

"We'll have to come back after school."

All through morning lessons Tim could think of nothing else, and as lunchtime approached he wondered if the thief was feeling hungry too, and might be sniffing around the oat-cake at that very moment.

'Surely he won't bother crash-diving into Sheriff's oats when there's a delicious takeaway meal just hanging there waiting to be grabbed and eaten?'

The afternoon lessons passed more slowly than ever.

The Dragon was doing her best to watch Tim carefully, as she had promised, so he couldn't day-dream as much as before. But, now that the new evacuees had squeezed into the classroom, even Mrs Low couldn't watch him all the time. So, under cover of the extra noise, he was whispering to the Cullen boys, explaining about his revolutionary rat-catching invention.

"You are not paying attention, Timothy Oliver...AGAIN!"

Mrs Low had noticed that his mind was on other things, and he spent the rest of the afternoon standing in the corner, studying the wall.

Four o'clock came at last, and the rat-catchers ran back to Crab Mill, straight into the barn and up the ladder. In the gloomy light they saw that the box had fallen off its prop, and was lying, face-down, on the floor.

Joe hesitated, then walked across and tapped the top of the box.

Immediately there was a violent movement inside. The two-penny robber was trapped alright. But now they had a problem.

"Who's going to pull him out?" asked Tim.

They looked at each other. Neither was keen on the idea of an angry rat taking a chunk out of his finger.

"It's your invention, Tim, so p'raps you should." Joe grinned.

"But it's your farm, Joe, and your rat, too, in a way…so p'raps you should." Tim grinned back.

Then he noticed some old sacks lying in a corner and remembered the notice, with a rat caught in a net. He picked one up.

"If I hold the open-end over the door, Joe, and you slide it back, he'll jump through the hole to escape and straight into the sack."

"Good idea, Tim!"

They checked that there were no holes in the sack; then with shaky hands, Tim held it up to the doorway. Joe's hands were also shaking as he slid the door back, and in a flash, a fat brown body sprang through the hole and into the sack.

"Got 'im, Joe!" cried Tim in triumph, quickly closing the neck of the sack.

"Now all we need is his tail," said Joe. "But how can we get that?"

Tim thought about the three blind mice who had their tails cut off by the farmer's wife with a carving knife. But this was no mouse! It was a rat…a big, angry one, and he was sure that Joe's Mum wouldn't want to tangle with it. It certainly wasn't blind, judging by its aerobatics, and they could easily imagine two rows of very sharp teeth looking for tender young fingers.

They needed help.

They picked up the sack and went to find Gerry.

"So your trap worked! Well done, lads."

"But we've got to take his tail to Constable Lewis for the reward," Tim explained, "and we don't know how to."

Gerry smiled.

"You leave that to me. You'll have your tail before I go home!"

Half an hour later there was a knock on the back door. It was Gerry holding out a long, dripping rat's tail. The boys were curious.

"Thanks Gerry," said Joe, "but how did you do it?"

"Just a heavy stone and a bucket of water."

Tim pulled a face.

"You mean you drowned it?"

"That's the way we do it in the country, Tim. It's kinder than poisonin' 'em or catchin' 'em in a trap!"

The city boy wasn't so sure.

On their way back from school the next day, they called at Constable Lewis's house which was the Police Station, to present him with their trophy, and tell the story.

"A tale of a tail! Well done, lads!" he smiled and handed over two pence.

"That's from the government."

Joe sighed. "Pity we can't spend it on extra sweets."

****

Tim was enjoying the life of a farm boy now. The end of lessons couldn't come too soon, and he and Joe usually ran most of the way back to Crab Mill. Better still, if Sheriff had been working in the big field and had finished, they would 'hitch' a lift back to the farm, sitting astride the giant horse's broad back, enjoying the aerial view over the high hedges, feeling his great strength, and swaying from side to side in time with his steady, rhythmical plod. It was graceful and soothing after a hard day in the Dragon's den. Sheriff was the perfect transport. There was no need for petrol or oil or air for tyres – or tyres for that matter. Just Joe's daily feeding, watering and grooming. He never broke down, and guaranteed to deliver them, in his own time and at his own pace, back to the farm.

"And I bet he dunna' even notice that you're on his back!" said Bob.

CHAPTER EIGHTEEN

BIKES AND BRIDGES

It's true that, just occasionally, Tim felt a bit home-sick for his City. The grand buildings in the centre, and the big shops; the Pier Head with its trade-mark Liver Buildings and floating pier receiving and despatching the squat, crowded ferries to and fro across the river; mountainous liners and cargo boats, reminders of what had made it a world-famous city, nudged in and out of mile after mile of docks by fleets of tugs; and, everywhere, the powerful (Tim might have said 'intoxicating' if he had known the word) scent of the sea.

Yes, he missed the grandeur and the 'buzz'. But it was humbler, everyday things much closer to home that he missed most...the newspaper-stand by the railway station, where he bought his Beano and read the headline news; the grocer's shop on the opposite corner where, before the war, a whole bag of broken biscuits cost a penny; the strangely named 'MYSTERY', a vast, bleak 'prairie' of playing fields with nothing but football pitches as far as the eye could see - a footballer's paradise; the tiny sweet shop on Penny Lane where, if he was willing to take a chance, he could choose a number on a board, hoping to win something worth more than the penny he had handed over. Even better; the shabby but friendly 'Grand' Cinema, and best of all, a free ring-side seat to watch the 'Scot' rush past. Yes, even if it was crowded, noisy and smoky, city life was very interesting. And it was 'home', if only a distant memory.

Colemere was very different, but very interesting too, Tim thought. There was the soft multi-greenness wherever you looked, instead of the monotone red brick of endless houses; the cathedral-like silence of the woods with their giant elms, beeches and oaks - as stately as any of the grand columns of the city-centre, but unspoilt by the smoke of thousands of chimneys - a perfect auditorium for the innumerable bird inhabitants to show-off their songs, or for echoing the excited voices of children playing hide and seek; the awesome stillness and smoothness of the mere, perfectly mirroring the fringe of trees at its edges, ideal for 'ducks-and-drakes' and a free bathe in warm weather; the overarching blueness of the sky on sunny days, and the quiet, daily routine of the farm, where people and animals hardly ever seemed to be in a hurry.

Yes. Mrs Fowkes was right. Life in the countryside was much more peaceful than in the big city, and safer, too. For one thing there were no buses or trams, and hardly a motor car for miles; just the odd tractor trundling along. So it was safe for cycling, and Tim was desperate to learn.

There was only one bike at Crab Mill, which belonged to Joe's Dad. Joe had learnt to ride on it, and he said he was sure his Dad wouldn't mind if Tim did, too.

It was an old Raleigh, made for riding around farms and country lanes, not for speed; but that didn't bother Tim. As long as it had wheels, a seat, pedals and handlebars, it was 'fine'. But Mr Everson's bike had one special feature. When war was declared he had bought a new front lamp and was very proud of it. It had a mask fitted over the beam, with a slit, so that only a very thin line of light would shine on the road and be unseen from the air.

Mrs Everson said that that wasn't really necessary, as he never went out on it at night, '...and in any case, a German bomber would hardly bother to drop a bomb on a cyclist in the middle of nowhere!'

"But the government says that all vehicles must have front lamp-covers," he insisted, "and my bike is a vehicle, so it must have one. We must obey the wartime rules!"

Mrs Everson didn't argue.

One misty, autumn Saturday morning, the boys pushed the

Raleigh up the lane to the village pump. The top lane was a good place for learners. It sloped downwards steadily from the pump, and ran for about three hundred yards to a T junction. There were no 'tight' bends to negotiate or tricky hills to climb.

"First we'd better try it for size," said Joe.

There was a stone next to the pump, which riders used to mount their horses. Tim climbed onto the stone, then onto the bike; but, as Joe had expected, his feet hardly reached the pedals, so he had to get off, while Joe did a bit of tinkering with a spanner.

The seat was lowered, and Tim got back on.

"Now," said Joe, "bring one pedal up to just past 12 o'clock, and when you're ready, push down on it…then you'll start movin', and when the other pedal comes up to the top and starts goin' down, push down on that one…and just keep doin' that – there's nothin' to it, really."

"But how do I keep my balance? I dunna' want to fall off!"

"Once you're movin' it's easy," said the teacher. "Just keep lookin' straight ahead and pedallin'…and move the handle-bars a bit – that helps…and anyway, I'll walk along with you."

Tim did as Joe had said. He took a deep breath, pushed down on the pedal, and rider and bike began to move forward slowly. The road was level for the first few yards and he felt fairly confident, especially with his friend walking alongside holding onto the saddle. Then, as the bike went down the first bit of the slope, he began to feel more confident.

"You're right, Joe, there's nothing to it!"

He pushed a bit harder on the pedals and the bike duly went faster.

"How am I doing?" he asked, but there was no reply. He glanced down to check that his teacher was still holding the bike steady, but he wasn't there.

"JOE!" he shouted.

But Joe was a long way back, standing in the middle of the road, grinning.

"YOU'RE DOIN' FINE." he shouted. "JUST KEEP PEDALLIN'!"

So Tim kept pedalling and, to his surprise, he found that the harder he pedalled the straighter he seemed to go; and he had forgotten all about keeping his balance. It was just happening. Then he remembered Joe saying that it helps to move the handlebars about a bit, so he did, and started zigzagging slightly down the road.

By now the hedges were going past quickly, so he thought he'd better slow down; but Joe hadn't said anything about slowing down or stopping, and a question flew into his mind...

'Does Joe's Dad's bike have brakes; and, if so, how do they work?' He wished he'd asked before he got on.

Mrs Owens in Holly Cottage was in the middle of washing up the breakfast dishes, and as she looked out of the kitchen window she saw what looked like a very pale face travelling quickly along the top of her front hedge.

'That's strange,' she thought. She dried her hands and ran outside, almost bumping into Joe, who had only just remembered that he hadn't told Tim how to stop, or that there was a very large oak tree at the T junction which he should avoid, if possible.

By now Tim had almost reached the junction and spotted the oak coming quickly towards him. He made a quick decision that it would probably be wise to stop pedalling altogether, which was a good idea, because he needed to concentrate on avoiding the tree.

On the far side of the junction there was a grassy bank sloping up to the oak and, as the bike hurtled towards it, he gritted his teeth, let go of the handle bars and launched himself onto the bank, while the bike ran straight ahead into the tree. There was a dull, crunching noise, followed by silence, except for the sound of the front wheel continuing to spin around.

He lay on the bank for a few moments wondering if he had broken any bones, but didn't think he had. He was more worried about the bike. He could see that the handle bars were out of line, but otherwise there was no damage – except for Joe's Dad's wartime-

model headlamp, which had changed shape.

At that moment Joe ran up.

"Sorry, Tim," he said. "You were doin' so well, I thought you didn't need any help...but I should've told you how to stop."

Tim smiled faintly.

"That's alright, Joe. I dunna' think I've broken anything ... and I can ride now!" He uttered a faint "Yippee!" which seemed to tire him, because he lay back on the bank. Then after a few moments he propped himself up on one elbow and looked at the bike.

"But your Dad wunna' be pleased when he sees his headlamp!"

Mrs Owens was the next to arrive, puffing. She had heard the crash and hurried back into the house for her first-aid kit, although she was quite sure she would have to send for an ambulance.

"I'm fine, thank you, Mrs Owens," said Tim, "...just one or two bruises, I think." He groaned slightly.

"Well, you must come and have a drink of cold, sweet tea," she said. "You're probably in shock."

Tim didn't feel 'in shock'; just a bit dizzy; but, to please her, he said he would go. And, to tell the truth, he was quite enjoying all the sudden attention.

Joe took a few moments to straighten the handlebars, and they followed the village's Florence Nightingale back to her cottage, where Tim duly drank the tea which, she assured him, was the proper treatment for a case of shock. Then she said he'd better rest for a while, with a glass of her home-made 'pick-me-up', a powerful mixture of dandelion-and-burdock and extra-strong, crab-apple cordial. So it wasn't long before his face had returned to its usual colour.

They thanked Mrs Owens for the first-aid and set off slowly back to Crab Mill, Joe holding Tim steady with one hand and the bike with the other.

They found Joe's Dad in the tool shed, and Joe told the story of how Tim had 'daringly dived' onto the bank 'to save the bike from even worse damage', which kindly Mr Everson pretended to believe. Tim said he was 'really sorry' about the lamp, and was sure his Dad would buy a new one to replace it.

****

It was Shirley's 11th birthday on November 25th and Mum and Dad had bought her a bike. It was supposed to be a great secret, and had been carefully wrapped up, which Tim thought was a waste of paper as well as time, because, as soon as Dad took it out of the taxi, everyone could guess what it was.

When it was unpacked, they all went to admire it and watch Shirley doing circuits around the lower yard. Then, as Mrs Everson had prepared a birthday tea, the bike was left propped up against the pump while they went indoors…all except Tim who, of course, had recently become a cyclist himself, and hung around for a few minutes to examine the birthday present.

Unlike Joe's Dad's bike, it was streamlined, and its dark-green paintwork gleamed in the sunshine. In fact every part of it gleamed, and Tim wanted more than anything to have a ride on it. He measured himself against the seat which was only slightly too high for someone of his size; but he was sure it would do. Now he just needed to choose the right time to ask.

All the next morning he was very polite to his sister and even combed his hair, before asking if he could possibly 'have a little ride' on her bike, to show everyone that he could cycle, too.

"You can, Tim," she said, "as long as you promise to be careful with it," which he earnestly did.

Mum and Dad had stayed the night at a Guest House in Ellesmere, and came for lunch at Crab Mill.

"If Joe's Dad will let me borrow his bike," Dad said, "I'll go with you, Tim," which was probably a polite way of saying that it mightn't be a good idea for Tim to go for a ride on his sister's new bike all by himself.

So it was arranged. Tim had a practice ride around the lower yard to make sure he hadn't forgotten how, and, after a wobble or two, set off with Dad towards the canal path, which they chose because it was level. The paths along the side of the Shropshire Union Canal were ordinary bridle-paths in the grassy verge, except under the bridges where there were cobbles, with ridges to help the horses pulling barges to get a good foothold. They were fine for horses and walkers, but cyclists had to be prepared for a very bumpy ride.

"Be very careful going under the bridges, Tim," Dad said, as they made their way down from the road to the canal path. "The roofs are quite low, so keep your head well down over the handle-bars and your eyes straight ahead. Don't look up at the wall and, whatever you do, don't look down at the water."

Tim nodded, and began to feel nervous.

For the first part of the ride the canal ran in gentle curves along the far side of the mere, with only the wood in between. Dad went ahead at a slowish pace and Tim rang the bell every so often, to let him know that he was keeping up. The sun filtered through the trees, making patterns on the bank, and he was enjoying being in charge of the new bike. He wasn't at all nervous now. Bowling along on the shiny, brand new bike, with the wind in his hair and boldly ringing the bell, he felt like Toad of Toad Hall.

Everything went well at the first and second bridges, although he didn't like the ridges and the jolting. They overtook a group of wild ducks paddling peacefully in the same direction. An elderly water rat which had just emerged from its hole in the canal bank, glanced up at the young cyclist and scurried back to safety, as if it sensed that something unusual might be about to happen.

It was when they reached the third bridge that things began to go wrong. For some strange reason the jolting seemed much worse, and instead of keeping his eyes straight ahead, he looked up at the wall very close to his head, then down at the cold, dark water, and toppled in, head-first, followed by Shirley's bike.

There was a great splash, and after a few seconds, a watery shout ..."HELP!"

Dad, who was about thirty yards ahead, leapt off his bike and

dashed back to the bridge where Tim had just come up for air. He grabbed him by his shirt-collar and, with a great upwards tug, hoisted him out of the water and onto the cobbles. The canal was always deepest and muddiest under the bridges, and the bike had sunk without trace. In the meantime the ducks had gone into reverse and were heading back the way they had come.

Tim stood dripping and shivering under the bridge, wondering how he would tell Shirley that he had lost her new bike, when a voice came from overhead.

"Hello, down there!" Then the speaker came running down to the footpath. She was wearing extra-long Wellington boots, and Tim guessed that she was used to people falling into the canal. When she saw him she laughed.

"Hello! Couldn't you be bothered putting your swimming trunks on?"

Tim smiled faintly and went on dripping and shivering.

"Well, you chose a good place to fall in." She pointed to a house on the far bank. "That's my house. You'd better come with me and get those wet things off, before you catch your death of cold. I'll find you some dry ones. My son's about your size, so that shouldn't be too difficult."

"I'm Mary Clemson," she said to Tim's Dad. "I was in the garden when I heard the splash and the shout. He's not the first person to fall in here. It's those ridges. Nobody likes them. Oh, by the way, we've got a boat-hook to fish the bike out."

Tim noticed a rowing boat tied up to the canal bank.

"I'm Tom Oliver," Tim's Dad said, "and the almost-drowned rat here is my son, Tim."

Mrs Clemson led the way up over the bridge to her house. Tim's Dad found the boat-hook and went fishing for the submerged bike. It had settled down on its side in the mud; but, before long it was back on the path. There was a bit of mud on the brakes and mudguards, and the bell didn't sound much like a bell. Otherwise it was as good as new.

Tim was soon dried and dressed and sipping a hot drink. They thanked the kind hostess, and promised to bring the borrowed clothes back the next day. Then they crossed over the bridge to cycle back to Crab Mill, except that, at the bridges, Tim got off and pushed. He was taking no chances.

When they reached Fowkes' bridge they stopped for a short rest, and Tim wanted to talk.

"At the cinema it said we won the Battle of Britain, Dad, so why are the bombers still coming? I heard Mr Everson telling Gerry that he watches them on clear nights."

"Well, you don't usually win a war by winning one battle, Tim, although it was a very important one. If the Luftwaffe had won, Hitler would probably have sent his armies across the Channel. Instead, our fighter-pilots sent his air-force packing. But he knows that, as long as we're free and can fight back, we're a danger to him. That's why those bombers are still coming over. He couldn't beat us in the air, so now he's targeting the factories in our biggest cities, to stop us making weapons and planes, so that we'll have nothing to fight with. He wants to put our sea-ports out of action, too. That's why I can't come to see you and Shirley very often."

He looked at his watch.

"Come on...I'll race you to the boathouse!"

They wheeled the bikes as far as the wood path. Tim was given a start, and raced along, his head low over the handlebars, to reach the boathouse just ahead and triumphantly ringing the bell, which had dried out and sounded like a bell again; although he did wonder if Dad had really tried.

Back at Crab Mill they told the story of Tim's sudden dip, in a way that made everyone feel sorry for 'poor Tim', including Shirley, who said he could borrow her bike again, 'as long as you keep away from canals'.

The next day all the family walked as far as the third bridge, where Tim told his story again in great, dramatic detail, adding some made-up bits, such as how it felt to be rescued by his Dad 'just as I was going down for the third time'.

Then they crossed the bridge to hand over the borrowed clothes and say 'Thank you' again. But, as usual, time was fast running out. They retraced their steps back to the farm. Then, just as they were getting used to being together as a family, it was time for Mum and Dad to head back to the black-out and the blitz.

****

A letter from 6, Welbeck Avenue
December 8th 1940.

Dear Shirley and Tim,

Thank you for your letters. The bombers don't come every night, but now we know they might, we can be ready to go to our safe place in the shelter. It's more comfy now, with bits of carpet on the floor and even some pictures on the walls. So you mustn't worry. Everyone is quite cheerful. Hitler doesn't realise how stubborn and brave people can be when they're fighting for their freedom!

It won't be safe for you to come home for Christmas, so we will be coming to Crab Mill Farm instead. We'll be staying at the Kestertons Guest House. It will probably be full of evacuees' Mums and Dads! Mr and Mrs Everson have invited us for lunch on Christmas Day.

Love, Mum and Dad

PS. Have a lovely Christmas party, and don't get too excited, Tim!

CHAPTER NINETEEN

A PARTY

The kind ladies of the Colemere Mothers' Union organised a party in the boathouse. It was for all the village children, but especially for the evacuees who couldn't go back home for Christmas, and everyone was asked to go in fancy dress. Mum had made Shirley a 'Florence Nightingale' nurse's uniform, Muriel was going as 'Alice in Wonderland' and Joe was the 'Lone Ranger'. Tim wanted to be the 'Spy in Black', but Mrs Everson said that he couldn't very well go as a Nazi officer, so he agreed to be Peter Pan instead.

It was already dark as they set off from the farm, and icy cold. They pulled their collars well up under their chins as Joe led the way with his torch, down through the frosty carpet of beech leaves. The residents of the wood had already settled down for the night, the mere was very still and peaceful, and the full moon was perfectly matched by its reflection on the surface. In the moonlight, the black and white of the boathouse made it stand out against the starry sky.

Old Sam was waiting at the door to welcome everyone. He was 'Father Christmas' for the evening, with a cotton wool moustache and beard, and a red coat and hood; and, although everyone except the very youngest knew it was Sam, because of his bright eyes and voice, they pretended that they didn't, and shook hands politely.

The party-room ran the whole length of the upstairs and was decorated with miles of paper-chains which the pupils had made in school on the last day of term. Sam had made sure that there was lots of holly and mistletoe everywhere. He had brought a giant-size Christmas tree from the wood, and the ladies had painted cones to hang on it. They had been busy all afternoon making the wartime rations go a long way, and at one end of the room a table was laid out with delicious food.

The postmistress was there, and the vicar and Mrs Pye, who was in charge of the games. She had been a gym teacher in her younger days and had an unusually loud voice.

The party began with musical chairs. At first there was a lot of pushing and shoving, and Mrs Pye had to raise her voice to remind the boys to 'behave like gentlemen, please', which most of them found very difficult. Tim and Joe stayed in until there were only six left. Then Leslie Hinton and Tim tried to push each other off the last empty chair and Leslie won, so Tim was 'out'. James Pye was the next out, then Leslie, and then Sheila Cullen. That left Joe and Hilary, to decide the winner.

A chair was placed at each end to make it fair, with just the one in the middle. The music started and the two finalists circled the chairs twice, watching each other carefully and slowing down each time they approached the middle chair.

When the music stopped, Joe was behind Hilary and needed to get past; but as well as being quite quick on her feet, Hilary was a stocky girl, and stuck her elbows out, so he couldn't. There was a people-jam coming around the end chair and Joe still couldn't push past, so Hilary got to the middle chair first and flopped down as the winner.

Joe smiled like a good sport, and Hilary, who liked Joe, offered to share the prize, which was a packet of boiled sweets.

"You can have some when the party's over, Joe," she said sweetly.

"No thanks," said Joe. "I don't like boiled sweets."

"That's not true!" Muriel whispered to Shirley. "He loves boiled sweets, but Hilary keeps her sweets in a pocket in her knickers and they get warm and sticky. That's what he doesn't like!"

The next game was 'Pass the Parcel' for the small children, and there was a bit of trouble when Mrs Hughes' grandson, Nigel ('Nipper') Hughes, who was determined to get one of the prizes, refused to pass the parcel to the next child until he had taken a piece of wrapping paper off, even though the music hadn't stopped. An awkward situation was only just avoided when his Grandma whispered something about 'chocolate' in his ear. Then, reluctantly, he passed the parcel to the next child. Later on he did have a turn at opening the parcel and won a prize, which was just as well, the vicar said to Grandma, as there might have been a scene if he didn't win something.

Then it was time for tea. There was a name on each place, and next to Tim was the pretty girl he had seen in the church choir. The name on her place was Margaret and, as they sat down, she smiled and said "Hello, Tim. I saw you in church." Tim blushed and said a quiet "Hello, Margaret."

Joe was sitting next to the vicar's wife who kept calling him 'Joseph', probably because it was nearly Christmas, he thought.

By this time they were all hungry and ready to tuck in, but first the vicar said a rather long 'Grace', thanking God for a safe place to live in, when thousands of people have lost their home in the bombing...for this lovely food when so many people in the world are hungry,...and for sending us our very own evacuees who can't be at home with their Mums and Dads this Christmas...et cetera, et cetera. Grace finally came to an end, everyone said a loud and grateful 'AMEN!' and reached for the sandwiches, followed by sausage-rolls, and cup-cakes; and Tim and Joe ate at least three jelly-creams each.

Then Father Christmas made his entrance with a bulging sack of presents and when Tim went forward to receive his, he winked.

"A Happy Christmas, young Liverpudlian!" he whispered. "A sea-story for a seaside lad!"

Tim grinned. "Thanks, Sam...I mean Father Christmas!"

Back in his seat he looked at his present. It was a sea adventure story, 'Mr Midshipman Easy', by Captain Marryat, which was just the kind of story he loved.

The last item on the programme was the fancy-dress competition. Mrs Pye, the Postmistress and Father Christmas were the judges, and they awarded the boys' prize to Keith Cullen as Robin Hood, and the

girl's prize to Shirley as Florence Nightingale. Tim guessed that they knew how much she would miss her home at Christmas, and hoped it would cheer her up.

The party ended promptly at seven, the vicar thanked the ladies for 'a super party' and Sam for being 'a perfect host', and the children set out for home through the quiet darkness with cries of 'Happy Christmas!'

****

On Christmas morning Tim woke very early, as usual, and in the half-light he could just see the outline of an extra-large stocking with mysterious bulges at the end of his bed. He felt down to the toe, and, hidden in the very tip was a silver sixpenny 'tanner'; then he pulled out a toffee apple, followed by a bar of 'Five Boys' and a bag of toffee. There was an adventure story 'The Coral Island', and an album for cigarette cards, with two sets of 'Famous Footballers'. He did a quick check to make sure that Dixie Dean was there.

By now Joe was awake too, with his mouth full of toffee and busy examining his stocking. There was an adventure story for him, too, 'Treasure Island', and an album, with two sets of cigarette cards of British ships and planes.

Mum and Dad had made sure that the boys were treated equally.

It was the evacuees' first Crab Mill Christmas, and when they went downstairs, there were specially noisy cries of 'Merry Christmas!'

Breakfast had just ended when there was the sound of a car bumping down the lane, and after a quick ''scuse me!' Tim was the first to the garden gate to meet Mum and Dad. Shirley followed, and the four hugged as if they hadn't seen each other for ages.

There was no talk of bombing and war. It was Christmas, and soon it was time for church. Mr Everson had gone ahead to ring the bell, the church council having decided that 'the people of Colemere and Lyneal will not let Adolf Hitler and his nasty gang stop them celebrating Christmas in a proper manner,' and Constable Lewis had agreed.

At the far end of the mere Mrs Fowkes smiled at the sound skimming over the still surface to reach her cottage. She put on her shawl and bonnet, picked up her well-used prayer book and set off through the wood in good time to take her usual seat next to the font.

The church was full again and looking especially beautiful, as country churches do at Christmas, decorated with holly, ivy and mistletoe; and Sam had transferred the party tree from the boathouse to stand next to the pulpit with a large star at the top. Lots of children were there, excited and noisy, the smaller ones holding tight to a doll or toy. Nipper Hughes had brought his favourite present, a kids-sized trumpet, which he was determined to play during quieter parts of the service, until his Dad confiscated it.

Tim spotted Margaret on the front row of the choir and thought she looked his way and smiled during the prayers, when their eyes were supposed to be closed.

In his sermon the vicar talked about the Wise Men from the East.

"... those three brave men who refused to obey the tyrant, King Herod, and betray the baby Jesus, just as we won't bow down to the Nazi dictator."

After *'O come, all ye faithful'* and a warm handshake from Mr and Mrs Pye, everyone filed out cheerfully into the cold air and headed home for Christmas lunch.

The Mums and girls made their way back up to Crab Mill while the boys took Tim's Dad to the hideout. He was very impressed.

"Now it needs trip-wires and cans...that sort of thing, to give a warning if a stranger or an enemy is approaching."

Tim and Joe looked at each other and nodded; then they headed back to the farm for Christmas lunch.

Tim's chickens had been spared because of their important role in the war-effort, but two of the ducks were out of luck. They were followed by Christmas pudding, doused in brandy and set alight by Joe.

After lunch the two families stayed at the table listening to the King's Christmas message on the wireless. He sounded more like a King this time, Tim thought. More certain. He had been walking around the streets with the Queen after the bombing, in and out of mounds of rubble, chatting to people. Everywhere they went, crowds came out to cheer and wave. They were grateful that their King and Queen and the princesses had stayed in London to share the dangers

of the Blitz with them.

Now, as people up and down the land sat around wirelesses listening, everyone felt that the King was their friend, not just a distant person on a throne. He spoke about the cruelty of the bombing and the bravery of the nurses, doctors and ambulance men; and, when he mentioned the 'courageous fire-fighters', Tim hoped he might include the 'vigilant fire-watchers', but guessed that he couldn't mention everyone who was doing brave things.

When he had finished speaking, they stood up to sing 'God save the King'. Tim didn't know all the words but hummed the tune.

Then it was time for presents. There was a pair of gloves and a 500 piece jig-saw puzzle for Muriel. For Joe there was a Dandy Annual and a dart-board.

For Shirley there was an embroidery set, the Girls Crystal Annual, and some school stories from Grandparents, aunts and uncles.

For Tim there was a model of the Hurricane fighter-plane to go with his Spitfire, a Beano Annual and yet another bag of sweets from Auntie May, generously saved from her ration.

The time passed quickly – much too quickly for the evacuees, and the taxi arrived to take Mum and Dad back to Ellesmere for the night, before they returned to Liverpool the next morning.

After the extra-long day and all the excitement, Tim was very tired, and went to bed before Joe; but instead of turning the light on, he stood at the window looking out at the sky. It was empty, except for the stars. On this special night at least, Hitler's bombers were leaving the world in peace, and Tim remembered the carol – 'Silent night, holy night'. The vicar had said that it was a 'German carol', and Tim thought about his Mum and Dad going back to the danger, and wondered why everything had gone so wrong in the world.

CHAPTER TWENTY

SLIPPING AND SLIDING

The Christmas holidays ended, but the winter wouldn't go away. Grandma Oliver was right. Shropshire could be bitterly cold in winter, and Tim was especially grateful for his brightly-coloured mittens as he trudged up The Drive to school.

Mr Everson complained that the ground was 'as hard as iron', and there were flurries of snow in the air. The cows spent most of the time in the sheds, and even the chickens preferred to stay indoors.

Then, one morning, Tim woke up with a start. It wasn't because he heard a noise. It was the very opposite. There were none of the usual sounds...animals' hooves in the yard, a milk-churn being rolled along. Nothing. Just an eerie silence, and a lot of light.

He got up to look out of the window and there was the answer to the mystery – SNOW!

He shook Joe.

"Come and look, Joe!"

Joe opened one eye, blinked in the brightness, then jumped out of bed and ran across to the window. He looked down into the yard where the ice on the water trough was piled high with snow.

"It must be a foot deep!" he gasped, hopefully.

They washed and dressed in record time and hurried downstairs.

"You boys'll be happy to hear that school is closed today," said Mrs Everson, smiling.

They couldn't believe their luck – NO SCHOOL and LOADS OF SNOW!

They gobbled down their porridge, which tasted better than

ever; then Joe said he would pluck up his courage and go with Tim to deliver Mrs Fowkes' milk.

The old lady was surprised.

"Well, well! If it inna' that noisy Joe Everson bringin' my milk for me. I never thought I'd see you walkin' up my path, Joe. But I'm glad to see you. Perhaps we can be friends now. And well done, Tim! I thought I mightna' be gettin' my milk at all today. I reckon that's worth two biscuits each!"

She noticed that Tim was cupping his hands and blowing warm air in.

"I see our city boy's gettin' tougher, Joe!"

They left her making her cup of tea, and ploughed their way back along the wood path, munching their reward for braving the snow.

"She inna' so fierce, after all," said Joe. "I'll try to be quieter in future…and I wunna' call her names any more!"

Through the trees they could easily see the mere. It was completely iced over, with a smooth covering of snow, like a vast white table-cloth. A group of young ducks had crash-landed in the middle with a great fuss.

Joe laughed. "I think they're tryin' to work out where the water's gone!"

Their morning jobs didn't take long. The chickens didn't seem to know what to make of the snow and had opted to stay in the hen house where it was warm, so the collector's job was easy. Sheriff was covered with his winter jacket and, apart from his daily feed, didn't need much attention from his groom. So the boys were free, and Joe led the way to the barn to rescue the family sledge from the cobwebs and dust.

It was a three-seater, designed and built out of solid oak by Joe's Grandfather. They lowered it slowly from its hook on the wall.

"It's a monster!" Tim cried, "and so heavy."

"It's a dead weight now," said Joe, "but just wait 'til it's runnin' on the snow!"

He fetched some candle stubs from the kitchen to wax the runners. Then they tugged it across the lower yard and were puffing their way slowly up the lane, when they heard a shout.

It was Joe's Dad.

"Dunna' forget how fast that fellow can move, Joe, specially with three passengers on board...and steer 'im carefully. He's got a mind of his own!"

"Dunna' worry, Dad," Joe shouted. "I can handle 'im."

Tim smiled, listening to Joe and his Dad talking about a sledge as if it was human.

It took all their strength to haul the monster up the lane to the top road, but once on the level it moved almost by itself. In the dips they had to run to keep up, and soon reached the mere-field bank. Most of the Colemere kids were there, and quite a few from Lyneal had waded down The Drive to join in the fun. Tim caught sight of

Charlie and his gang and decided to keep out of their way. The bank already looked like railway sidings, criss-crossed by dozens of sledge tracks.

They got ready for a trial run with Joe up-front holding the guide-ropes. He pointed the sledge so that, at the bottom of the bank, it would run safely alongside the mere.

Pushing with their heels, they inched forward onto the slope, picked up speed quickly and swept past smaller sledges. Joe was holding them on course quite confidently, and as the slope levelled out, they slowed to a gentle halt.

"Wow, Joe," Tim gasped, "that was amazing! But we must make sure we dunna' run onto the ice."

"Dunna' worry, Tim," Joe laughed. "I can manage him!"

Back at the top Joe spotted Geoff.

"Hi, Geoff!" he yelled. "Want a ride on the Crab Mill Express? There's space for one more at the back."

"You bet!" Geoff yelled back and hurried over. "I'll push to get us moving."

They pulled the sledge well back from the top of the bank so that Geoff could get up speed, and Joe positioned the sledge in the same groove as on the first run.

"Let's go!" shouted Geoff and pushed them across the ridge, jumping on just in time to take his place at the back as they went over onto the slope and grabbing hold of Tim, who was holding very tight onto Joe.

Then, quite suddenly, the monster seemed to take over. The runners jumped out of the tracks Joe had chosen, they changed direction and hurtled down the steepest part of the bank towards the icy mere.

Joe tugged on the ropes to try to get back on the right course, but it made no difference as they raced across the level ground and onto the ice, which was perfect for sliding.

Joe's face turned pale under his freckles.

"We've got to stop!" he yelled.

Snow particles flew up into their faces as they tried to dig their heels into the ice, but it made no difference. They weren't slowing down. They were heading at speed straight for the middle.

By now most of the other sledgers had stopped and were standing, open-mouthed, watching the Crab Mill Express heading further and further from safety.

Muriel and Shirley ran down to the mere-edge, staring anxiously after them, Shirley wondering if she would ever see her brother again, and wishing she hadn't been so bossy, and Muriel thinking about the ticking-off she would give to Joe. After all he was in charge.

One of the Lyneal lads was already running towards the boathouse to tell old Sam that there was an emergency, and that 'some rope and a ladder might be needed'. To everyone's surprise it was Charlie.

Back on the ice, Joe remembered that Sam had said that it was always thickest at the edge; but how thick was it in the middle... and would it take the weight of Joe's Grandad's sledge with the three lads on board? He tugged on the rope until his knuckles turned white under the skin. Geoff had closed his eyes and was trying to remember a prayer, and Tim was wondering if he was about to meet Jenny Greenteeth and hear the mystery bells after all. They knew that they were in great danger and dug their heels harder into the ice in one last, frantic effort to stop.

At first it seemed to make no difference, but at long last the monster took pity on its passengers, slowed down and came to a halt only forty or so yards from the buoy marking the middle and deepest part of the mere.

They sat there quietly, not daring to move. Joe was trembling; so was Geoff. Tim thought he might have wet his pants.

"Get off carefully," whispered Joe, as if a loud word might crack the ice and make it open up and swallow them.

They stood up, tugged the sledge around, and started tip-toeing back the way they had come. Their leg muscles were aching and it was difficult to get a grip on the ice; but at last they reached the waiting crowd and everyone cheered. Muriel reserved Joe's ticking-off until they were back safely at the farm, and hugged him instead. Shirley hugged Tim, which was very unusual.

Some of the other lads were dragging the sledge up onto the bank when Sam arrived with Charlie, carrying ropes and a ladder, and ready with one of his speeches. He was bright red in the face, and looked more cross than Joe had ever seen him. He glared at the three.

"DIDNA' I TELL YOU TO KEEP TO THE EDGE?" he barked.

Joe tried to explain. "But Sam, I couldna' steer…and then we couldna' stop." But the old chap took no notice. He turned and stared at the crowd, and his eyes looked wider than ever. They were all his kids, in a way, as Joe had said, and he hated the idea of any of them being harmed, especially on his precious mere.

"YOU MUST LEARN THE LESSON! If you want to go onto the ice, KEEP CLOSE TO THE EDGE!"

The crowd stood quietly, while the three adventurers, who didn't need the lecture, went across to their old friend. Joe knew Sam best and spoke for them all.

"We're really sorry, Sam."

The old chap mumbled something about 'lads!', then picked up the rope and ladder and trudged off towards the boathouse.

For the trio, that was the end of sledging for the day. They had been seriously scared, and the last thing they wanted to do was to get back on the Joe's sledge. They also had some unfinished business.

Muriel had told Joe about Charlie running for help. He was standing with Jerry and Reggie, and the three walked over to them.

"Thanks, Charlie," said Joe "... that was quick thinking."

Charlie shrugged. "I didna' want you to go under the ice, that's all...and anyway, me and my gang want to be friends in future." Jerry gave a toothy grin and Reggie said "Yeah!"

"Us too," said Joe, and Geoff and Tim nodded.

Then they escorted the sledge back to its resting place in the barn. Tim was the last out, and as he was closing the door he remembered what Joe's Dad had said.

'That fellow's got a mind of his own.'

He stopped for a moment to glance back at the monster resting innocently on the wall, then shut the door quickly and hurried after Joe.

After lunch the boys were back at the scene of the morning's adventures, but without the 'Express'. They decided that it was safer to slide on their feet. Sam had said that it was quite safe at the edge, even for a crowd.

James had already started a slide-path and said he would be the leader. The others lined up behind him in a queue – Muriel, who liked James, then Shirley and Hilary; Geoff came next, then the Egerton girls, then Don's big brother Robert. Joe and Tim formed the tail.

"Tally ho!" yelled James, and dashed down the slope followed by the queue, across the level ground onto the slide-path. Arms flapped about, but everyone reached the end safely, and was soon scrambling back up the bank for another turn. Now the slide-path was like glass.

This time they started from higher up the bank to get up even more speed, and the long line of sliders, with James in the lead, was gliding quickly and gracefully across the ice when a loud voice called from the direction of the vicarage...

"JAMES!"

It was his Mum, and James glanced over his shoulder. In a split second he lost his balance, arms waving wildly, and crashed down onto the ice. Muriel tripped over James, Shirley couldn't change direction and fell over Muriel, and one after another the whole line fell over in a giggling heap on the ice. Nobody was hurt and they were soon heading even further up the bank for another slide. Robert Williams took over as leader while James, who was a bit annoyed with his Mum, went over to demand what she wanted.

She was laughing.

"I only wanted to tell you not to fall over, as you were the leader!"

The sliding went on until they could hardly see the slide-path, so there were more pile-ups before everyone headed for home, tired-out.

****

The snowy weather wasn't only good news for sledgers and sliders. The air–raids had stopped. Joe's Dad explained that bomb-aimers can't locate their targets if the weather's bad. So the brave folk of Welbeck Avenue could spend the cold nights in their warm homes instead of huddled together in the draughty shelter.

CHAPTER TWENTY-ONE

DIG FOR VICTORY!

The snow stayed around for weeks. There were no more days off school, which Tim thought was a bit mean; but after school there was a rush to the mere-field, and the bank was alive again with sledgers and sliders, until the snow turned to slush and disappeared altogether.

The filigree frame of trees around the mere was turning green, and the wood came alive with noisy bird-song. After the long, hard winter, life at Crab Mill farm was extra busy, and the chickens were out scouting for new hiding-places for their precious eggs, to keep the young collector guessing.

But now that the weather was better and the skies clearer, the bombers were flying again.

"It's an ill wind that blows nobody any good," Mr Everson muttered, as he watched the night-raiders flying north. "Now they can pick out their targets..." But he kept his thoughts to himself.

Tim's Dad had extra fire-watching duties now, so it was usually Mum who came to visit, sometimes just for a day, but always armed with a supply of comics and sweets saved from her own and Dad's ration. There was lots to talk about, such as what Billy and the Dovedale Road lads had been getting up to in Wrexham which, Mr Davies said, was 'a much noisier place nowadays!'

But the few hours always flew by too quickly.

A week-end visit was much better. Mrs Everson kindly 'made up' a bed for Mum in the living room, and they could all have breakfast together. Tim always asked if she would like to do 'a bit of egg-collecting' with him, and once or twice arranged for her to 'accidentally' find a hidden cache of eggs.

Sometimes she went with him on his milk-run. Mrs Fowkes didn't have much 'grown-up' company, and insisted on giving her a cup of tea, made with the fresh milk, and one of her fruit biscuit 'specials', while she chattered on about the 'brave city folk'. To cheer his Mum up, she always said what a good milkman Tim was, 'hardly ever late, and always with a perfect layer of cream!'

On sunny afternoons they rambled in the woods or along the canal, Tim on the look-out for a rabbit or pigeon to shoot at with his catie, which had been returned to him with suitable warnings; and Shirley hunting for wild spring flowers for Mum to take back to Dad. They had usually wilted by the time they reached Welbeck Avenue, but to him they were 'as beautiful as a spray of orchids!'

A special treat was to catch the bus into Ellesmere on a Saturday afternoon for a Charlie Chaplin or Laurel and Hardy film 'matinee' at the Town Hall; or just gazing wishfully into shop windows, although there wasn't much to see, now that almost everything was rationed.

There was great excitement when Dad was given time-off from fire-watching for a week-end visit with Mum. On a warm afternoon they could take a punt out on the mere for a couple of hours, for Mum and Shirley to chat in the sunshine, and Dad and Tim to 'drop a worm in', hoping to land a good-sized perch or roach and, when they were in luck, presenting it to Mrs Everson to serve up for breakfast the next morning.

But always, the longer they stayed the harder it was to say good-bye, waving like mad until their arms ached and Mum's ginger feather was out of sight, then trudging slowly back to the farm, Shirley crying quietly, and Tim head-down, kicking the stones.

****

The Easter holidays arrived at last, and Mrs Everson asked for volunteers to help with the kitchen garden.

"We canna' fight, but we can 'dig for victory', that's what

Mr Churchill says. We must use every spare inch of our garden to grow food, or there wunna' be enough to go around."

Tim wasn't very keen on gardening. He couldn't be bothered planting things and waiting for them to grow. But Mrs Everson had said it was an emergency, and 'digging for victory' sounded like something worth doing. So the next morning he lined up with the girls and Joe, to be told what to do.

"Now, does anyone have a favourite vegetable they would like to grow?" Mrs Everson asked, and after a bit of discussion the girls chose beans and peas, Joe decided to try lettuces, and Tim agreed to plant a couple of rows of carrots.

"Dad says that the night-fighter pilots eat lots of carrots so they can see better in the dark,...so they must be good for us."

They collected the garden tools from the shed and set to work preparing the soil, planting the seeds and watering them. The girls wrote out cards to say what the seeds were, where they were planted, and who had planted them. Tim and Joe cut some hazel twigs and split the ends to hold the cards.

They had done their digging for victory and now the boys could concentrate on another important bit of war-effort – an early-warning 'system' for the hideout, which Tim's Dad had mentioned. Joe's

Dad's Home Guard hand-book had a chapter entitled 'Early-warning Systems for use on the Field of Battle'. It wasn't exactly what they had in mind, but there were a few helpful diagrams, which gave them one or two ideas.

The first stop was the tool shed, to locate a length of wire, and in a return raid on the wood they cut some more hazel twigs, about twelve inches long. Then they helped themselves to a few tin cans from the village 'mountain' and stones from the churchyard path.

Tim grinned.

"I'm sure the vicar wanna' mind, if we tell him they could help to save lives!"

At the hideout they stuck the hazel twigs in a semi-circle among the bushes, about thirty yards from the cave, put the stones in the cans, tied the cans to the ends of the wire and covered them with moss. Then they ran the wire along the tops of the sticks so that an unwary intruder would trip over the wire, the cans would rattle and the boys would have time to get away.

"We need to test it now," said Joe. "But we canna' do that ourselves, 'cos we know where the wire is."

"But the girls don't," said Tim, "and if they hear that we've got a secret den, I bet they'll try to find it. Let's give them some easy clues, so they can test it for us!"

That afternoon Muriel was doing her piano practice in the sitting room, and Shirley was pottering around in the kitchen, while Mrs Everson was rolling out some pastry.

Joe strolled in.

"Tim an' me've got a secret hideout, Mum," he said in a loud whisper. "It's in the wood just below the ridge, not far from Fowkes' cottage. No one'll ever find it."

Shirley heard every word, and hurried to tell Muriel.

"Let's have some fun, and go and find their so-secret hide-out!"

Muriel was glad of a reason to stop practising Chopin, and when the boys went across to the stable pretending to be feeding Sheriff, the girls slipped out of the back door and set off to the wood. Tim saw them go, and grinned.

"It's working!"

They waited for a few minutes, then took a short-cut along the ridge and dropped down to the hideout, to sit and wait.

It was almost tea-time when they heard voices among the trees and, suddenly, there was a loud rattling sound, followed by a scream. The boys emerged from the hide-out and grinned down at the girls.

"Welcome to our hideout!"

"That was a mean trick!" Shirley said. Her muddy hands and knees showed that she was the one who had tripped over the wire.

"Sorry, Shirley!" said Joe. "We didna' want to scare you. We just needed someone to test our warning system. But now you know where our hideout is, you munna' tell anyone. We can hide here if the Nazis ever come looking for us."

Muriel laughed.

"I dunna' think they would bother looking for two school-boys."

"Well," said Tim, "Eli told us that lots of children have had to hide from the Nasties, don't you remember...and that was in their own country!"

****

The boys spent most of the holidays at the hideout.

"We should have a Union Jack," said Joe. "It's a bit complicated, getting all the crosses in the right place, but there's a picture in Dad's Home-Guard book. We could copy that."

They pestered Joe's Mum to look out some white material and, after hours of hard work with Tim's box of paints, a rather patchy Union Jack was hanging proudly at the end of Joe's fighting stick, at the entrance to the cave.

Some days they took a packed lunch and stayed until it was time to do their jobs. It was a good place to watch the other residents in the wood. A family of grey squirrels had set up home in a hollow

elm tree close by, and seemed quite happy to have these unusual neighbours. They scampered up and down and from branch to branch, chattering at them. Sometimes the boys left a few hazel nuts, 'borrowed' from the Crab Mill pantry, just outside the entrance, as a token of friendship, and all that was left when they came back were empty shells.

If they sat very still just inside the entrance, they could watch foxes heading for the ridge on the look-out for rabbits, and the occasional badger glancing up at the hideout as it snuffled past in the evening dusk.

****

On Easter Day, the parish church was a sea of daffodils, and packed out. Even Charlie, who didn't go to church very often, was there with his Dad, taking up at least three places between them. Tim was disappointed to notice that Margaret wasn't in her usual place, brightening up the choir. 'She's probably visiting some needy old person', he thought.

The vicar was in good form again, reminding everyone that 'knowing you are standing up for the right against the wrong always makes you strong'.

Now Mr Everson was keeping tuned-in to the news on the wireless, and on evenings when he was out training with the Home-Guard, the boys took it over to the cowsheds where it was quiet. They perched themselves on milking stools and twiddled the dials, listening out for bits of news about the war, while the cows munched in their stalls.

There was bad news and good news.

The bombers were still pounding the big cities, and in the first few days of May they made the their heaviest raids ever, especially on London. Thousands of buildings were destroyed, fires raged all through the night, and hundreds of ordinary citizens were killed. It was Hitler's last desperate effort to make Britain give in, but it failed.

There was good news on the high seas, too. The battleship Bismarck, the 'flag ship' of the German navy, which had been bossing the seas, was cornered by British destroyers. Its rudder had been badly damaged, so it would have to stand and fight.

The boys ran across the yard to spread the news and, when they got to school the next morning, everybody was talking about 'The Bismarck'.

Archie had brought a picture.

"It's like a floating mountain!" said Ted.

"Or an ogre," added Betty, "stomping about, frightening everybody!".

After supper that evening everyone at Crab Mill gathered around the wireless listening in to the latest news bulletin. The reader sounded excited...

"This morning, the German battleship Bismarck was attacked and sunk by British destroyers and Swordfish aircraft."

Everyone cheered, and the next morning Archie was very popular with his picture.

"Imagine THAT sinking!" said Ted.

Now the last thing Tim wanted to think about was arithmetic, which was the first lesson. Why couldn't they have a history lesson, if possible one about destroyers and battleships and swordfish aircraft? He wanted to concentrate on the Bismarck, not long division. After all, Joe and he were the first to hear the news. They knew the facts.

Unfortunately Tim couldn't keep the 'facts' to himself and he was whispering to Archie as Mrs Low was writing sums on the blackboard.

"The rudder was damaged ... that's why it couldn't get away...it was just going around in circles...SERVES THE BULLY RIGHT!" He checked that the Headmistress was still busy writing, and whispered on...

"...it was the 'tin fish' that sank it...they're the torpedoes that the Swordfish planes drop."

"TIMOTHY OLIVER!" Mrs Low had spotted them.

"You are not paying attention...AGAIN! And you are distracting Archibald."

"Yes, miss. Sorry miss."

"And how many times must I tell you that I AM NOT MISS? I might be 'Miss' in Liverpool, but in Lyneal I am MRS LOW!"

"Yes, miss."

****

"How can I please Mrs Low?"

The boys were on their way down The Drive after school, and Tim was troubled. On this day of glory for the British navy, he had been at war with the Headmistress again.

"Well, you could try harder, Tim," said Joe. "That's what your

Mum said. Don't you remember? 'Teachers always like pupils who try hard.'"

"But what if the lessons anna' interesting…like last week when we went to the mere to study pond-life, and we had to see who could find the most water-bugs. We all knew Hilary would win, 'cos she always wins, so I couldna' be bothered. I just got my feet wet and my socks smelly!"

They walked on in silence.

"You could volunteer to take Mrs Low her morning cup of tea."

"But that's Sheila's job…and anyway, you know what Hilary would say." He picked up an imaginary tray.

'Here's your morning tea, Mrs Low'.

'Thank you so much, Timothy'.

'How much milk, Mrs Low – just a dash? And how many sugars? Four lumps? Sorry, Mrs Low, you can only have one, 'cos sugar's rationed now, you know!'

No! There was no way he would ever consider being Mrs Low's tea-boy. Sheila's job was safe.

But what else could he do to win the Headmistress's smile? They sat on the jetty and talked about all the other jobs that keen pupils volunteer for. There was 'blackboard' monitor; that was cleaning the blackboard at the end of lessons and being covered with chalk dust. Tim didn't like that idea.

The milk monitor's job might be more enjoyable. If there was a bottle left over, the monitor was allowed to drink it. But that wouldn't be a treat to Tim, who could drink as much milk as he wanted, back at Crab Mill Farm; and in any case, collecting the 'empties' afterwards always left your fingers sticky and smelly. That was ruled out.

"You could ask to be moved to the front of the class. Then you'd have to pay attention!"

"But Hilary would still poke fun at me."

"'How am I behaving, Mrs Low?'… 'aren't I paying attention, Mrs Low?'… 'did you notice that I answered one or two questions?'… 'aren't I a good little evacuee, Mrs Low?'"

"NO! I certainly wunna' do that."

The outlook was bleak.

****

"Here is the eight o'clock news.'

The reader's voice echoed around the cow-shed as the boys sat gnawing at lumps of sugar beet.

'Germany has attacked its main ally, Soviet Russia.'

When Joe's Dad got home from shooting practice they told him the news.

"That's a big mistake," said the farmer. "Hitler should remember what happened when Emperor Napoleon of France attacked Russia. He got a bloody nose!"

CHAPTER TWENTY-TWO

THE PRIZE

The Headmistress seemed quite excited when she came into class two one morning.

"The School Inspector will be here tomorrow to test you on your knowledge of the Bible, and he will be awarding certificates to the best pupils. So I want you to look as smart as possible, and to be on your very best behaviour. We want him to get a good impression of our little school, don't we?"

She stopped speaking and frowned, as if something was bothering her. Then she looked at Tim, who was sitting comfortably at the back of the class thinking about battleships, and pointed to a desk right at the front in the middle.

"I don't suppose you've read the Bible very much, Timothy, but we can't have you not paying attention when the Inspector's asking his questions, so you had better sit here at the front. You can change places with Donald."

Don Williams had always wanted to sit at the back of the class. He grinned and took Tim's place quickly, before the Headmistress could change her mind. Tim trudged to the front and took Don's place.

The next morning, after assembly, class two filed into the classroom and took their places, with Tim at the front in the middle. After a few minutes the Headmistress came in with the Inspector, an elderly gentleman with white hair and a kind, grandfatherly look.

" Now children, this is Mr Belford our school Inspector, who will ask you some questions about the Bible," she announced importantly.

"Good morning, girls and boys," the Inspector began,

holding up a book which looked as if it had been taken in and out of schools for many years.

"When our brave King was crowned George the Sixth in Westminster Abbey, a minister of the church presented a Bible to him, and said 'This is the most precious thing in the world.'"

'That's interesting,' thought Tim, who would have said gold or jewels.

"Now," the Inspector continued, "can anyone tell me why the Bible is so precious?"

Everyone chewed their lip and tried to look thoughtful. For a long time nobody spoke and then, just when it seemed that the Inspector had got off to a bad start, Hilary, who was the cleverest in the class said "Is it because it's Holy, sir?"

"That is quite right," said the Inspector, "...and can you tell us why the Bible is called Holy?"

Now Hilary's brain was working overtime, and after thinking for a few moments, she replied "Is it because it's all about God and how he wants us to keep His commandments and be happy?"

Mr Belford was impressed.

"That is a very good answer, young lady." He looked at the Headmistress and beamed. Mrs Low beamed back, everyone nodded, as if they had known the answer all along, and Hilary sat down with a contented smile.

"Well now," the Inspector continued, "let's see what Bible stories you know."

Now it was true that Tim hadn't read the Bible very much; but, as we have noticed, he loved going to the cinema, and every Wednesday after school there was a children's film-show at the little chapel just around the corner from Welbeck Avenue. They were slides, not 'movies', but better than nothing, according to Tim, and it was free. Some kindly, elderly ladies served biscuits and drinks at the end, and he hardly ever missed.

He always enjoyed the miracles, such as the feeding of the five thousand and people being miraculously healed; and he thought the parables, like the Good Samaritan and the Prodigal Son, were really good stories. But his favourite ones were Joseph and his multi-coloured coat, David and Goliath, Daniel in the lions' den and other adventures, and he was hoping that the Inspector would ask about them. But he didn't. Tim guessed that that was because he thought everyone would know them off by heart, and wouldn't need testing on them.

But he badly wanted to win one of the certificates, to please the Headmistress and make her like the evacuees more, and while Hilary was impressing the Inspector with all her knowledge, he had been thinking hard. He worked it out that, when there's a test, being at the front of the class wasn't such a bad thing after all. School Inspectors have got to be fair and let the kids at the back of the class answer some questions. And, anyway, the kids at the front wouldn't be there if they weren't keen.

That was his way of thinking and he hoped he was right, because each time a question was asked, he put up his hand, but not too eagerly, hoping that the Inspector wouldn't bother asking such a keen pupil for an answer, before he had tested all the others. Then all he needed was a question he could answer confidently.

It was very risky, but his plan seemed to be working. Eli, Hilary, and one or two of the others were keeping the Inspector happy with brilliant answers, and he heard Shirley reciting Mrs Ferguson's psalm about the shepherd and the valley of death. Even Don answered a question or two, but the test was nearly over, his arm was getting tired and, so far, he hadn't had much of an opportunity to shine.

Then he heard a name which he had heard before.

"Who was Zacchaeus?" the Inspector asked, and this was Tim's big chance.

He remembered the slide-show about the nasty tax-collector quite clearly, and now he waved his hand about so wildly under the Inspector's nose, he couldn't possibly ask anyone else for the answer. He smiled down at Tim.

"Well, you've been very patient. So tell us about Zacchaeus."

Tim stood up, and the Headmistress stiffened slightly in her seat.

"Please sir," he began, "Zacchaeus lived in Jericho...that's where the walls fell down, sir. Everybody hated him because he was a tax-collector, and they were cheats and traitors. Well, one day Jesus walked through the town and Zacchaeus was desperate to see him. But he was very small and it wasn't safe for him in the crowd anyway, so he climbed up a tree - it was a sycamore, sir - to get a good view."

"I see," said the Inspector, "and can you tell us any more about the unpopular tax-man?"

"Oh yes, sir," said Tim, who was beginning to feel like the preacher at the chapel. "When Jesus reached the tree, he looked up and spotted Zacchaeus. He seemed to know all about him because he called him by his name."

"Zacchaeus, hurry up and come down. Today I want to stay at your house."

Tim paused, and now everyone was staring at him.

"It was surprising that Jesus said that to someone everybody else hated, sir, but I think he knew Zachaeus could change. He didn't tell him to turn over a new leaf or anything. He left that to Zacchaeus... and it happened, sir! He climbed down in a hurry and took Jesus home for supper – or it might have been lunch – and after that he was a new person. He stopped cheating everyone, and gave most of his money away to the poor people."

Now the Headmistress was leaning forward, with her elbows on her desk and her chin on her hands, listening carefully, and the Inspector had perched himself on the edge of Tim's new desk, as if he was one of the class himself. Hilary could hardly believe her ears.

But Tim hadn't quite finished.

"The religious leaders didn't agree with Jesus going to the house of a tax-collector, sir; but Jesus told them that Zacchaeus was just the kind of person he had come to help most."

Then Tim stopped and sat down.

"Well, girls and boys," said the Inspector, beaming again, "I couldn't have told the story better myself, and I think that is a perfect way to end the test."

Tim had answered his question just in time, and the class filed out for play-time, leaving the Inspector to talk to the Headmistress.

"You have some very bright pupils, Mrs Low," he said. "I was especially impressed by the boy in the middle at the front, the one with the untidy hair...although I noticed that he doesn't speak much like Shropshire boys."

"Actually, Timothy Oliver is an evacuee," she replied.

"Well, you must be very happy to have such a bright and enthusiastic pupil coming so unexpectedly to your school. Perhaps, in a strange way, Adolf Hitler has done you a favour, Mrs Low!"

The Headmistress gasped.

"I...I hadn't thought of it like that...and I think you may be right."

She walked with the Inspector to his car; then, deep in thought, back to her office for a cup of strong tea.

After play-time Mrs Low was standing in the doorway as Tim came in from the playground.

"Well done, Timothy. I didn't think you knew so much about the Bible." She smiled in a surprised sort of way, as if she had guessed his secret.

Tim smiled back, and hoped that she hadn't.

Two weeks later the postman called at the school with a large envelope and, in assembly the next morning, the Headmistress was positively beaming.

"The Inspector has awarded six certificates for Bible Knowledge to our little school."

Everyone sat up hopefully, as Mrs Low read out the names of the winners.

"Donald Williams, Betty Egerton, Muriel Everson, Eli Fieldsend, Hilary Sykes,..." At this point the Headmistress stopped and looked at Tim who was in his usual place at the back, concentrating hard, with his fingers crossed, but had almost given up hope. She smiled.

"And the last certificate....is for you Timothy."

The six winners walked to the front to receive their certificate and everyone clapped.

"Well done, Timothy!" whispered Joe, and grinned as Tim walked past.

Back at his desk, Tim looked at his certificate. It had a coloured border with scenes from the Bible, including Daniel in the lions' den and Jesus calming a storm. At the top it said 'Certificate for Bible Knowledge', and underneath in large silvery letters...

PRESENTED TO TIMOTHY OLIVER, EVACUEE

and at the bottom the Inspector had signed his name with a flourish.

James Belford,
His Majesty's Inspector of Schools
24th June 1941

A letter to Liverpool.

Dear Mum and Dad,

A nice inspector came to school and gave us a test about the Bible and I won a certificate. I think Mrs Low was supprised. I hope she likes evacuees a bit more now. Joe's Dad made a frame for it so it can hang next to the Spitfire and hurricane. I hope the little chaple hasn't been bombed or anything. Please tell the Ladies I remmembered about Zakeus, and it helped me to win the certificate and say thank you for me.

Love, Tim

CHAPTER TWENTY-THREE

SPONGES AND SKITTLES

The parish church mid-summer fête was always the high-light of the year and, this year, the vicar was especially enthusiastic.

"It will help to brighten up these dark wartime days," he said, and the organising committee met to discuss how to make the 1941 version better than ever.

They decided that, as there were thirteen evacuees in the two villages – seven in Lyneal and six in Colemere – it would be a good idea to have some extra events, specially for children.

Mrs Everson was on the committee, and asked Shirley and Tim if they had any good ideas that evacuees would enjoy. So that evening they met up with Geoff in the upper yard, which was where they usually discussed important matters.

Shirley voted for a skittle alley, if Gerry could make some skittles from the wood pile. Geoff said that throwing a wet sponge at a well-known person is always fun. Tim's only idea was a 'penalty shoot-out' with his football.

The committee thought the ideas were 'wonderful', and, as committees usually do with suggestions that people make, they asked the evacuees to be in charge of organising them.

On the day, the sun shone perfectly, and from the fluttering bunting and loud buzz of chatter and laughter, the anglers sitting peacefully in the punts on the mere could tell that something special was happening at the vicarage.

Stalls were set out on the top lawn – for cakes and vegetables, books and bric-a-brac, which, Tim learnt, was just another name for boring odd and ends.

Mrs Fowkes had a stall all to herself, selling garden herbs, which were a speciality of hers. They had been hung up to dry in the cottage and smelt slightly of tobacco, but tasted alright if left to soak briefly in water.

Her other speciality was what she called her 'Woodland Cordial'. It was made from a secret recipe handed down through generations of the Fowkes family, using wild berries, plants and nuts, water drawn fresh from the ancient well in the garden and a good helping of gin. It was greenish in colour and there was a little glass for people to 'taste before buying'; but she didn't seem to be selling very much.

The LUCKY DIP was organised by the Postmistress, and, as it was in aid of the church's 'fund for war-refugees', she had saved 'some little things' from the village's sweet ration, wrapped them up and hidden them in a tub of sawdust as prizes. Unfortunately, grandson 'Nipper' was up to his tricks again. He had decided that the best way to find the most interesting prizes was to climb in, which wasn't allowed, and his Dad had to pull him out feet-first, covered in sawdust.

The COCONUT SHY was run by the Williams family, using turnips instead of coconuts, the ships having more important things to carry on the long, dangerous journey across the Atlantic. They tended to explode when someone scored a direct hit; but the farm had had a successful crop, so there were plenty in reserve as replacements; and, as Don explained, 'the cows and sheep can have a party with the left-overs!'

Shirley's SKITTLE ALLEY was laid out on the middle terrace. She and Muriel had painted Gerry's skittles to look like Nazi storm-troopers, with extra-large stomachs, so they were easier to knock over. The bowls were large ball-bearings from Charlie's Dad's smithy, and the prize for knocking more than three skittles over was one of Mrs Everson's ever-popular toffee apples.

Tim and Joe had hung a car tyre from a branch of the giant cedar tree, and a notice on the tree said:

Be a Dixie Dean

Shoot the ball through the tyre
and win your money back!

It was a half-penny-a-shot for children and a penny for adults, and there was always a queue of lads, and a few dads, who pretended they weren't really trying, but looked a bit annoyed with themselves when they missed.

Tim was busy giving advice to some budding centre-forwards, when he noticed that a girl had joined the queue. It was Margaret from the choir and he ran over.

"You can take the ball closer, Margaret, if you like."

"Thanks, Tim," she said, and he blushed again. "I'll be alright shooting from the same spot as everyone else."

She handed over her halfpenny, placed the ball on the spot, and stepped back a few paces. Then she ran up and kicked the ball clean through the centre of the tyre.

"That was AMAZING!" exclaimed Tim, as he handed over her halfpenny. "I didna' think girls were any good at football."

"Well, when you've got an uncle who played for Wolverhampton Wanderers, you can learn a lot," she smiled, and wandered off to knock over a few storm-troopers.

The vicar was wearing his cricket flannels and college cricket pullover, which, Mrs Everson noticed, was becoming a tighter fit each year, and his cap, a faded shade of maroon. He had rigged up a 'net' and was challenging 'all-comers' to bowl him out.

To repay their debt to the church-yard, Joe and Tim had reported to the vicarage the evening before the fete, to bowl a few 'overs' to him. Tim was quite impressed by his style, but every so often during the afternoon, there was a cheer from the direction of the cricket net, which told everyone that the vicar had taken his eye off the ball and the stumps had been flattened.

The LOB A SPONGE side-show was the most popular. As the church verger, Joe's Dad had agreed to sit behind a board with his

head sticking through a hole, to let people throw wet sponges at him. Mrs Everson had painted a little 'Adolf Hitler' moustache on his upper lip, although Geoff, who was in charge, wondered if the vicar might think it 'not very forgiving' to throw wet sponges at 'The Fuhrer'. The vicar laughed and said that he would like to be the first to throw, and on his second lob, the soggy sponge landed right on the verger's head. Everyone cheered and Mr Everson smiled bravely, as the moustache dribbled down his chin; but after twenty minutes of bombardment he decided it was time to retire. Constable Lewis very sportingly took his place, and straightaway there was a long queue of lads who had never been allowed to throw things at the village bobby.

At four o'clock exactly the vicar announced that 'the foot-races are about to start on the lower terrace'. Tim and Joe closed the penalty-shooting down, quickly counted up their takings, which came to eleven shillings and four pence, and joined the other kids.

In the fifty yards race Geoff won the under-12s, as everyone at Crab Mill expected; Eli won the Under 11s, ahead of George Hanson, and Hilary won the Under 10s just ahead of Tim, which upset him quite a lot. Pam Egerton had practised all week for the Under 7s egg and spoon race, and was in the lead when she dropped her egg, and was frantically scooping it up, when Ruth Williams, who had also been practising hard, dashed past to win.

Luckily for Joe, Geoff was his partner in the three-legged race, so he just held on tight as Geoff tore down the track, and they won quite easily. Joe said he didn't really deserve a winner's prize.

Tim laughed.

"Even Geoff couldn't win a three-legged race all by himself!"

Then it was the Dad's race, which everyone wanted to watch, and both sides of the track were lined with spectators. Joe's Dad lined up with the vicar, Leslie Hinton's Dad, Nipper's Dad, Len, and Constable Lewis, who had dried himself off, saying that he never wanted to see another sponge. The lads knew how fast he could run, because he had found Charlie and his chums raiding farmer Williams's orchard, and had nabbed them before they had even reached the gate.

At the last minute there was a late entry. Tim's Dad had just got off the 3.30p.m. bus from Ellesmere.

"You're just in time for the father's race, Mr Oliver," Mrs Everson called out.

"You'll run, won't you Dad?" Tim asked eagerly, and Mr Oliver nodded. He was feeling a bit tired after a long, slow journey, but he knew how disappointed Tim would be if he said 'no'. He took off his jacket, and tucked his trousers into the tops of his socks.

Tim nudged Joe.

"Just watch, Joe" he said. "My Dad used to be on the wing for the Old Boys' football team, and he's fast!"

Mrs Pye was the starter, and had a bit of difficulty making sure that all the toes, especially the vicar's, were behind the starting line.

She raised her handkerchief and her voice...

"ON YOUR MARKS...GET SET...GO!" She dropped the handkerchief, the crowd cheered, and the line of Dads rushed forward. Just as the lads had expected, Constable Lewis got away to a quick start and was in the lead at the halfway mark, with Nipper's Dad and Tim's Dad just behind. There was a bit of (accidental) elbowing, then twenty yards from the tape, Tim's Dad surged ahead and won by a yard. Constable Lewis was second, Nipper's Dad third, and Leslie's Dad fourth. The vicar and the verger came in equal last; but, as someone pointed out, they had both been extra busy that afternoon. Amid all the excitement Joe noticed that Tim spent the next few minutes standing very close to his Dad.

The GRAND FINALE was the villages' tug-of-war. Each village was allowed to have twelve tuggers, three ladies, three girls, three lads and three men. The Colemere team were 'The Spitfires' (by special request of Tim) and the Lyneal team were the 'Hurricanes'

Mrs Hughes, the Postmistress, who was quite stocky, was one of the Colemere ladies, with Joe's Mum, who was also stocky, and Mrs Owens, from Holly Cottage. The men were Tom Brown, Bob from Crab Mill Farm, and Mrs Fowkes' son John. Muriel, Ruth Hinton and Hilary formed the girls' section. The boys were James, Joe and Brian Cullen. Tim was left out because he was 'a bit lightweight'.

When the Lyneal team lined up, Tim noticed that pretty Margaret was one of the girls, although he thought she might be a bit too dainty for a tug-of-war. Then he spotted Charlie and his Dad jogging up and down, flexing their muscles.

"Oh no!"

Old Sam was the referee. In his much younger, stronger days he had tugged for the famous 'Wimpey' team, and looked splendid in his striped jacket and scarlet-peaked cap with a large 'W' on the front.

The teams stood with six tuggers on each side of the rope.

"TAKE THE STRAIN!" shouted Sam. Hands were licked, the rope gripped tightly and heels dug in.

"HEAVE!" and the tugging began.

The Lyneal and Colemere folk gathered near their teams; shouting "H-E-A-VE!" and "P-U-LL!", "Come on Hurricanes!", and "Go for it Spitfires!", and for a minute or so the red rag marking the exact middle of the rope stayed quite still over the centre line. Then, inch by inch, it moved towards the Lyneal line, as the Colemere team began to tire, lungs bursting, and teeth gritted. Tim dashed across

and yelled 'Dig your heels in!" and "Pull together, Spitfires!" But it
was no good. The Hurricanes had too much muscle. Charlie and his
Dad were just leaning back, as if it was all too easy, and although the
Spitfires made a last desperate effort, the red rag hovered just for a
moment before edging over the Lyneal line. Sam raised his arm and
pointed to the Lyneal team as the winners. The Lyneal supporters
cheered wildly, and Charlie flexed his muscles again for everyone to
admire.

Old Sam presented the 'trophy' to Charlie's Dad as the
Hurricanes' captain. It was a silver cup which a previous vicar
had won, rather luckily, it was said, for catching a pike in a fishing
competition on the mere. He had dozed off in the warm sunshine
and woke up in time to find the unfortunate pike, a fifteen-pounder,
towing the punt slowly to safety in the reeds, and so tired after such
an effort, the vicar had landed it quite easily.

Mr Smythe held the cup up for the crowd to see, and very
sportingly said "Well pulled, Colemere!" before posing for a
photograph with Charlie.

That brought the fête to a close and the crowds spilled out in
all directions, laden with plants, cakes, books and comics, herbs,
woodland cordial, lucky-dip prizes and boring odds and ends from
the bric-a-brac stall, leaving the vicar and the committee to clear up,
and the patient anglers out on the mere in peace at last.

In the warm late-afternoon sunshine, three figures made their
way slowly across the mere-field towards Crab Mill Farm – a tired
Dad and on either side a proud evacuee. Now they would have him
all to themselves for a whole day, and they both wanted badly to be
the one to carry his suitcase. Shirley said she should do it because she
was the oldest. Tim said he should, because he was the youngest - and,
anyway, he was the strongest, or so he thought. A serious squabble
was only just avoided by Dad deciding that Shirley should carry it as
far as the boathouse, and Tim the rest of the way.

They stopped for a few minutes and sat on the jetty, one of

Dad's favourite places, and chatted.

The docks had been badly bombed again during the May raids, but had been repaired in record time and were shipping thousands of soldiers and aeroplanes overseas, and unloading the convoys bringing food aid from America and the Empire.

"There's been no sign of any bombers for a few weeks," said Dad. "They're too busy bashing the Ruskies!"

Shirley looked hopeful.

"Does that mean we can come home?"

"Once we're quite sure they aren't coming back. So try to be patient, Shirley, and wait a little while longer."

CHAPTER TWENTY-FOUR

HOME AGAIN, AGAIN

Every morning, now, Shirley was up early and watching out for the postman. If he arrived before it was time to leave for school, she was the one who reached the garden gate first to meet him, quickly flicking through the mail.

If he didn't come before they left for school, her first question when they got home was always 'Is there any post?'

But the days went by, it was more than a week since Dad had visited, and still there was no news from home.

Then, at last, a letter arrived. It was from Mum, and Shirley tore it open.

'The bombers have done their worst,' it said, 'and we think they've given up. So we'll be coming down at the end of term to bring you home.'

She ran to tell Tim.

"We're going home, Tim, and this time we're staying!"

But Tim was mixed up again, and went up to the top yard to be with his chickens and think. He was happy being a country lad, with Joe and his family. He was even quite happy at school now. He had been promoted to the second row from the front of the class, and Mrs Low had also asked him to be what she called the museum 'curator'.

But deep down he missed his Mum and Dad more than ever, and it was getting harder to say 'good bye' when they visited. He was looking forward to being back with Billy and the others, too; playing footie and catching up on train numbers. Mum said that the 'Coronation Scot' was running as usual, so Mr Impitt's gloomy warning hadn't come true; and he was sure that there must still be lots of shrapnel lying about just waiting to be picked up by a keen hunter.

Geoff's Mum came to take him back to Stockton Heath. The Ship Canal had been bombed, as his Dad expected, and quite a lot of houses and shops had been knocked down. But now that the Luftwaffe was otherwise engaged, the ships were getting through safely.

Geoff came to Crab Mill Farm to say cheerio.

"Keep up your running, little steeplechaser!" he said to Tim. "Your legs are longer now and you're getting fast!"

Just before the end of term the committee held a final meeting at the museum. It had been set up in the shed at the end of the school yard and the exhibits were laid out on a large table. Eli's aunt Ruth had persuaded a friendly bin-man to save a few scraps of shrapnel for 'a special war museum in the country'. The boys said she was 'a real sport'. Ted's Dad had brought two smelly burnt-out incendiary bombs, although Tim said his Dad could have brought 'a truck-load'. Mrs Hughes had donated some boiled sweets and aniseed balls, which couldn't go mouldy, and they had saved the wrapper off a Five Boys bar, to show what a week's ration was. In the very centre of the table sat a lump of ugly Nazi bomb and a card which said...

An actual piece of the bomb which fell in the field next to the school. It flew into the school wall and was found in the playground by pupils of the school, including some evacuees.
September 1940

Pictures of fighters and bombers had been pinned on the walls, and Archie's picture of the Bismarck was there, with the word SUNK! in large letters underneath.

The girls had made a map of the two villages, with a piece of glass for the mere, some blue ribbon for the canal, and cotton-wool, coloured different shades of green, for the Colemere woods and The

Drive 'tunnel'. It was spread out on a table, with flags to show where the evacuees had stayed. Mrs Low, had played her part by searching out a map of England. It was very out of date, but showed the cities the evacuees had come from – Stoke, Birmingham, Manchester and Liverpool, and strips of tape linked them to Colemere and Lyneal.

Joe's Dad had brought some spare posters from the Home Guard headquarters, 'Careless talk costs lives', 'Dig for Victory', and one which said ...

'HITLER WILL SEND NO WARNINGS!
So always carry your gas mask with you!'

The boys thought it was funny, because nobody bothered, except Constable Lewis, who continued to carry his around with him everywhere, even on his bike, 'to set a good example!'

Now the committee stood quietly around the table...Joe, Ted, Don, Archie and Tim, and Eli had been invited because of Aunt Ruth's shrapnel.

"What'll happen to the museum when us evacuees have gone back home?" Ted asked.

"It should stay here," said Joe, "so kids in the future can learn what it was like to be in the war."

"And to be an evacuee," Tim added.

At play time on the last day of term most of the evacuees were busy saying goodbye to their school-friends.

Eli said that Aunt Ruth was coming the next day to take him back to Birmingham. The others asked if she had had news about his Mum and Dad.

"Just one letter," he said, sadly. "It said they were being sent to a special camp to work for the Fuhrer and I must not worry...but I do."

"Keep up your running, Eli," said Tim, to cheer him up. "Perhaps we'll run together in the Olympic Games one day."

"That would be good," he said, and smiled.

At the last assembly Mrs Low asked the evacuees who were going home to come out to the front. They stood in a line and she smiled at them.

"Children, we are very sorry to be saying goodbye to you. You have made our little school a more interesting place, and we are grateful. But now you will be with your parents and grandparents again, and we are happy for you. Please come back some day and see us again."

Everyone clapped and Miss Beddoes dabbed her eyes with her hanky.

At the end of lessons, Tim plucked up his courage and knocked on the kitchen door.

A familiar voice said "Come in!"

He gulped, pushed the door open, and stepped into the Headmistress's 'study'. Mrs Low was having her afternoon tea and when she saw it was Tim, she put her cup down and stood up.

"I've come to say goodbye, Mrs Low."

The Headmistress smiled sadly.

"When you came to Lyneal school, I thought that you and I might never be friends, Tim," she said and he grinned.

"...but I was wrong," she continued. "I didn't understand how difficult it might be for a city boy away from his mother and father to settle into a little country school like mine. But we're friends now, I hope, and I'm very sorry that you and Shirley are leaving us. I think you'll be safe in Liverpool now that the bombing has stopped, but I hope you will come and visit us again one day."

"I will, Mrs Low... Thank you for having me," he said and, in a strange way, he really meant it.

He was walking slowly across the playground and felt a touch on his shoulder. He turned and found Hilary, his old enemy, grinning at him...

"Cheer up, Tim Oliver!" she said. "You're going home! You

should be happy."

"I am, really."

"I'm sorry I was catty in class."

"I should have let you play football with us."

They stood there just looking at each other, wondering what to say next.

"Cheerio then, Tim."

"Cheerio, Hilary."

Joe was waiting for him at the school gate after school, and as they walked down The Drive, he could tell that his friend was feeling sad. Joe wasn't very happy either.

"I'm sorry you're going home, Tim. We've had a lot of fun."

"Yes."

They walked on without speaking.

After tea Tim ran down to the boathouse to see Sam.

"I thought you might be staying in Colemere for good, master Oliver," said the old chap. "You're getting to be a real Shropshire lad; but I wunna' forget you." He held out his hand.

"And I wunna' ever forget you, Sam," said Tim, and they shook hands, like men.

Tim cut across the mere-field to the vicarage.

"I'll keep my sword to remember you, Tim," said James "and how our square held against the Lyneal lads."

"Be careful what you shoot at with that catapult, Tim," said the vicar, "and keep asking those difficult questions!"

"I will, I promise!" Tim replied, and had just turned out of the drive to head for the village when he heard a loud, clear voice calling out...

"Farewell, Tim Oliver!" It was Mrs Pye, waving from the front door. "...and God bless you!" Tim waved back and headed up the bank to the Post Office.

"It's nearly two years since you first came into my Post Office, Tim," said the Postmistress, "and I was hoping you might be staying a bit longer. But it's best for you to be at home with your Mum and Dad, now that the raids have stopped. We'll miss you...and your pretty sister. You go on being brave...and come and see us again." She reached over the counter and put a large bar of 'Five Boys' into his hand.

"That's a bit extra to your ration, Tim. Mind you, not a word to anyone!" She winked.

"Oh, thank you, Mrs Hughes," he gasped, and thinking he might start to cry, he turned, ran out of the door and headed back to the farm, leaving behind him the smell of liquorice and the bell tinkling faintly.

After their jobs the boys ran through the wood to the hideout. They made a pact to meet there again 'next year in the summer holidays'. Joe promised to check the early-warning system every now and again, 'in case the foxes or badgers have been playing games with it', and Tim waved 'cheerio' to the squirrel family.

The next morning he delivered Mrs Fowkes' milk for the last time.

"I'm going home tomorrow, Mrs Fowkes," he said sadly.

The old lady put her hands on her hips, and frowned a big frown.

"And I thought you were stayin' here for good, my young friend! Well, my cup o' tea wonna' taste as good ever again!" she said, and, before he could escape, she bent down and hugged him so hard he could hardly breathe. Then she stood at the cottage door, puffing away at her pipe and waving through a cloud of blue smoke, until the little milk-man disappeared from sight, the milk-can clinking, swallowed up by the wood.

Later that morning Mum and Dad arrived in Bill Brett's Morris, and there was a lot of talking. Mrs Everson said some nice things about Tim, not mentioning the times she had sent him back to the

bathroom to wash his neck properly.

"He dunna' like soap much!" she smiled.

Mr Everson said how well he had done as the egg-collector.

"He can sniff out a well-hidden nest as well as any weasel!"

Shirley and Muriel went to check the new garden. The peas and beans were growing nicely and Tim's carrots had been doing well, too, although the rabbits from the top field had helped themselves to a few when nobody was looking.

Then it was time to say 'Goodbye', which Tim wasn't looking forward to. He went over to Mrs Everson.

"Thank you, Mum," he said quietly. It was the first time he had called her that, and as they hugged, it was her turn to hold on for a long time.

He didn't hug Mr Everson. 'Men' didn't usually hug in those days.

"I'd like to be a farmer one day," he said, which was the best compliment he could have paid to his country Dad.

"You can come and practise at Crab Mill any time you want, Tim," he said. "I can find plenty for you to do, and I'm sure Joe will be glad to see you back."

Joe nodded vigorously.

Then they were off.

The Eversons stood in a sad little line, Mrs Everson wiping her eyes on her pinafore, and Muriel and Joe trying their best to smile, as the Morris made its creaky way up the lane.

In front, Bill Brett and Dad chatted about the war and the price of petrol. In the back seat, Shirley and Tim sat quietly, Shirley happier than she had been for two years, and Tim sad and happy at the same time. And in between, with her arms around them, sat Mum, who had made a new stylish hat with a greenish feather to celebrate their home-coming.

****

The Dovedale Road kids came back from Wales the next week, and soon Billy and Tim were back in their usual places on the end wall, armed with their train-spotters' note-books.

In between trains, Billy told his story from the day of Mrs Ferguson's bomb.

"We went back to Wrexham the next day," he said. "Mr and Mrs Davies said they were expecting me when the bombing started. One night, Mr Davies took us up a hill just outside the town and we could see the sky over Liverpool lit up by search-lights and huge clouds of orangey-coloured smoke from the fires started by the incendiary bombs. We could even hear the explosions and the ack-ack guns."

Mr Davies said he didn't want to frighten me.

"Just so that you can see how brave your Mum and Dad are," he said "...and how wise they were to send you to Wrexham."

He stopped speaking and had a dreamy look in his eye, as if he was watching it again. Then he went on, more cheerfully...

"We never got to play rugby as well as the Welsh lads, but when we played footie we beat 'em easily!"

"We had a great Christmas party at the school, and snow-ball fights against the Welsh kids. Owen's Dad took us to Crewe station one Saturday to spot some main-line trains. It looked funny painted all over, like a giant jig-saw puzzle, 'cos it would be a target for the bombers, Owen's Dad said. We weren't in time to see the 'Scot' go through, which was a pity; and we couldn't stay long, in case of an air-raid."

"When Mr Davidson told us we were going home, I was sorry in a way, specially saying good bye to Owen and Bronwen and their Mum and Dad. I was happy staying with them...I really felt like one of the family, like Mr Davies said. I said I'll go back to visit one day."

Then it was Tim's turn to talk about the 'Spy in Black', his unexpected dip in the canal, and the Christmas party. He described the adventure on the Colemere ice, and how he and Joe had made friends with Charlie Smythe. He thought he'd better not mention the adventures with the rabbits.

Now that the football season had started Tim was even looking forward to school. But he had spent too much time day-dreaming at Lyneal school, and struggled to keep up with the others.

Shirley should have started at her new school, Blackburne House, but she was ill and couldn't. The doctor said it was probably because she had been so worried about her Mum and Dad in the bombing, and 'perhaps being in charge of a very lively young brother'.

A year later she had recovered, and now she had another brother to cheer her up, Roger, ten years younger than Tim.

****

The next September, Tim started at the school where his father and grandfather had both been pupils. The Collegiate School was a majestic, castle-like edifice, built with the reddish sandstone on which the city had been built, like the Cathedral and most of the grand buildings in the city-centre.

To an evacuee coming back from a tiny country school, this one looked as if it had been built for giants, and Tim felt very small. The

sound of the voices and feet of a thousand lively boys echoing up and down the endless corridors and staircases was almost as scary as that of the 'gong' which reached every corner of the vast building to signal the end of lessons.

The sticky tape was everywhere still, and the air-raid shelter smelt as bad as ever. Tim's name was still on his bunk, and the Spitfire picture on the wall, like the Spitfire and Hurricane models over his bed, reminded him that the war was still going on.

Only now it was going on all over the world.

V FOR VICTORY!

The war went on for four more years and was fought on land, sea and in the air across every continent. By the end of 1941 the United States of America and Russia had joined Britain and her Empire against Germany and her allies, Italy and Japan, and, although it had been safe enough for Shirley and Tim to return home, the gas-masks stayed by the front door, and Tim checked his blackout every night.

But the 'tide of war' was turning, and soon it was the skies over Germany which were black with enemy bombers. Tim shuddered when he heard about 'fire-storms' destroying whole cities, and he thought about the German children. They would be the evacuees now.

Then at last came the news that Hitler was dead and Germany had surrendered. The war in Europe was over, and at midnight on May 7th 1945, the ships in the Mersey and ports all over Britain and Europe sounded their horns, three short and one long blast, the letter V for victory in Morse Code.

The next day was VICTORY IN EUROPE DAY.

In London the King and Queen and Princesses waved to the crowds from the balcony of Buckingham Palace, but it was the man with a 'bulldog' face standing with them whom the crowds had specially come to see and cheer – Winston Churchill, the British David, who had dared to stand up to the German Goliath and, with the help of brave allies, had won a great victory for freedom.

There were great celebrations in Liverpool, too. After London, it had been the Luftwaffe's favourite target. Time and time again its docks had been burnt down. At times it had seemed that it might not survive.

Now, with every other brave city, town and village up and down the country, it could share in the victory.

In Colemere, Joe and his Dad rang the church bell until their arms ached, and Charlie and his Dad took over, followed by Constable Lewis, who had finally donated his gas-mask to the school museum.

On the Crab Mill Farm piano Muriel played 'Land of hope and glory' for the umpteenth time, and Joe brought the Union Jack from the hideout to hang from the roof of the barn, which was the highest point in Crab Mill, where it was still flying, although very faded, when Tim came for a holiday the next summer.

Old Sam rooted around in the boathouse loft and found a very old Union Jack, dating, he said, from the Boer War, which needed some repairing as well as dusting. Then he rowed out and attached it to the mere-centre buoy where it bobbed about proudly in the breeze, before heading back to the boathouse to prepare to receive the village children for a Grand Victory Party.

Mrs Fowkes had invented a new variety of Fowkes' Woodland Cordial which she called her 'Victory Celebration Cordial', containing yet another 'secret ingredient', and Mrs Everson, Mrs Owens, alias Florence Nightingale, the Postmistress and the vicar's wife bravely accepted her invitation to come to her cottage that evening to toast Mr Churchill 'in proper style'.

At the vicarage, after putting in a guest-appearance for Welshampton Cricket Club in a celebration match against Wem Cricket Club, in which he took a respectable three wickets for the loss of only eighteen runs, the vicar settled down with a cup of tea to prepare his final wartime sermon, entitled 'More than conquerors!'

Meanwhile, up and down Welbeck Avenue flags fluttered excitedly in the warm summer breeze. Billy and Tim hung bunting between numbers 6 and 7. Mr Impitt had planted a pole in his front garden to fly the Union Jack, and the flag of St George and England was flying proudly from Mrs Ferguson's new upstairs window, where passers-by might just hear Henry holding forth from his new cage. The men were setting up tables all along the street for a tea party later in the day when Harry Simpson, who was home from the navy, would be the Guest of Honour.

School was closed for the day, and a very happy Tim Oliver, ex-evacuee, scrambled up on the end wall with Billy, to watch the 'Scot' go by right on time, and wave.

Tom Farrell was born and, apart from a two year break as a wartime evacuee, brought up in Liverpool. Educated at the Collegiate School and Loughborough College, he has a Bachelor of Divinity degree from London University. Before being ordained as a Church of England minister in 1971, he taught Physical Education and Religious Education in several schools, and represented Great Britain in the 1956 and 1960 Olympic Games. British 400 metres hurdles record holder for six years, Tom captained the British track and field team at the 1958 European Championships, and was chaplain to the British team at the ill-fated Munich Olympics. After ordination he served as a curate in Liverpool, chaplain at Dulwich College, vicar of Wonersh, a commuter village in Surrey, and Rector of St Margaret, Lothbury in the 'Square Mile'.

Married to Liz, with three children and nine grand children, and first cousin of Booker Prize winner J.G.Farrell, in retirement Tom still preaches and runs regularly.

Lightning Source UK Ltd.
Milton Keynes UK
UKOW050939110212

187106UK00002B/1/P